VIRAGO
MODERN CLASSICS
183

Elizabeth Taylor

Elizabeth Taylor (1912–1975) is increasingly being recognised as one of the best writers of the twentieth century. She wrote her first book, *At Mrs Lippincote's*, during the war while her husband was in the Royal Airforce, and this was followed by eleven further novels and a children's book, *Mossy Trotter*. Her short stories appeared in publications including *Vogue*, the *New Yorker* and *Harper's Bazaar*, and have been collected in five volumes. Rosamond Lehmann considered her writing 'sophisticated, sensitive and brilliantly amusing, with a kind of stripped, piercing feminine wit' and Kingsley Amis regarded her as 'one of the best English novelists born in this century'.

THE
WEDDING GROUP

Elizabeth Taylor

Introduced by Charlotte Mendelson

virago

VIRAGO

This edition published in 2010 by Virago Press

First published in Great Britain in 1968 by Chatto & Windus
First published by Virago Press 1995

A CIP catalogue record for this book
is available from the British Library.

ISBN 978-1-84408-655-9

Typeset in Goudy by M Rules
Printed and bound in Great Britain by
Clays Ltd, St Ives plc

Papers used by Virago are natural, renewable and
recyclable products sourced from well-managed forests and certified
in accordance with the rules of the Forest Stewardship Council.

Mixed Sources
Product group from well-managed
forests and other controlled sources
www.fsc.org Cert no. SGS-COC-004081
© 1996 Forest Stewardship Council

Virago Press
An imprint of
Little, Brown Book Group
100 Victoria Embankment
London EC4Y 0DY

An Hachette UK Company
www.hachette.co.uk

www.virago.co.uk

To Renny and Rosalind
Joanna and David

INTRODUCTION

Poor Elizabeth Taylor.

No wonder she needs an introduction. First, she was a publicity-shunning, pearls-wearing sweet-manufacturer's wife from Reading, who shared a name with a violet-eyed, multiply-married superstar. Second, her natural territory was domestic life, which has never been fashionable. Third, the titles of her books were mostly unworthy of her, prim and repressive. Is it any wonder that people hesitate to read her novels?

If only we could rename *The Wedding Group*. Elizabeth Taylor deserves so much more than semi-obscurity. She is seriously good. Indeed, she is the perfect mid-twentieth-century novelist: less dated than Ivy Compton-Burnett, less snobby than Dorothy L. Sayers, less given to occasional silliness, whisper it, than my beloved Iris Murdoch, against whom I will not usually hear a word. However, once a novelist excels at something – whether it is Austen with her small canvas or Murdoch with her bohemian monsters – she tends to be known and praised and then damned for it. Part of Taylor's problem is that, even in her lifetime, her novels, like the woman herself, were assumed – by those who did not actually know them – to be demure: too civilised to excite passion. This is quite wrong. Elizabeth Taylor was also a former member of the Communist party, and a governess; she had secrets, including a lover, which her friends continued to keep hidden after her death. She wasn't male, or from the upper- or working-classes, or insane or gay. Does that mean she couldn't write good fiction? If you think so, close this book.

So, in a parallel universe in which novelists receive exactly the fame they deserve, let us imagine that she has another name, and different titles. Will her twelve novels, her four volumes of stories, be taken seriously now? Be realistic. This is twenty-first century Britain, where feminism is derided almost to death and the private lives of women, including what Taylor called the art of motherhood, are treated with a contempt which our supposedly unenlightened ancestors could not have imagined. What hope is there for her stories of suppressed lust and quiet heartbreak, set against a backdrop of bread-and-butter pudding?

There is hope, because her characters are real. They live real life. And they suffer, because that is what people do.

The Wedding Group is a magnificent novel of loneliness and little lies. It begins with the unsatisfactory home-life of Cressy, granddaughter of one of the most insufferable artists ever to bestride a fictional world: preening Harry Bretton. Bretton is the founding patriarch of Quayne, an artistic family compound where his womenfolk bake bread 'on a large scale' and weave and, with careful expressions of 'pleased anticipation', listen to his views about Aquinas or his favourite subject, himself. Quayne is a monument to Bretton's ego. Taylor wrote exceptionally well about artists, but Bretton is particularly vile: Stanley Spencer crossed with Eric Gill (whom Taylor knew) but without the talent or, probably, the horrors: just an ordinary domestic monster, fat with self-love:

He crossed the studio to his unfinished painting of 'The Raising of Lazarus', and . . . pointed out to himself, as he might have done to a ring of admiring students, the organisation of the whole, the slanting, fore-shortened figures, and the richness of all the day-to-day textures that he loved so much – herring-boned tweeds and lumpy knitting-stitches and basket work and braided hair. Lazarus was in striped pyjamas, for he particularly liked painting striped pyjamas. He tried to concentrate on the picture . . . but other, extraneous thoughts came into his mind instead – the words 'Sir Harry Bretton', for instance. That he was *not* – and it would have sounded so well – was a grievance of long-standing.

Cressy rebels. Who could blame her? She escapes to a 'beautiful' room of her own, the fusty attic of extremely close antique-dealing siblings, where she lives in poverty on baked beans and processed – not homemade – cheese, delighting in the modern world of which she has so long been deprived. There is beauty at Quayne, but she does not want it: 'the cabbages were curled and purple and full of raindrops, and their leaves creaked stiffly as Mo [her cousin] held them in her arms.' Meanwhile, in a big house full of flowers and antiques and modern art, the ageing, sprightly, desperate Midge prepares *poulet à l'estragon* and *crème brulée* for David, her spoilt journalist son, and devotes herself to keeping him so happy that he never wants to move out and leave her alone.

No other novelist would have handled what ensues with such restraint. In *The Wedding Group*, unlike some of Elizabeth Taylor's other novels, there is no crashing melodrama; no wars or fires. Nobody murders Midge or walks in on antiquarian incest or leaves anyone else, although the threat is there. Instead, Taylor deploys her knowledge of how little we know ourselves and others – 'no one can misunderstand a mother so completely as her own children' – to illustrate the worlds of pain behind the expensive curtains: the endless little tragedies of parenthood, marriage, old age. *The Wedding Group* is full of sadness, particularly loneliness: the kind so bad that it can be eased by the sight of an empty lit-up bus, or an uninhabited room. 'A long emptiness before her, and all the days the same.'

Yet Taylor does not pile on the suffering, or strain to make us sympathise with her feckless, selfish protagonists, with her tearfully pushy adolescents or manipulative parents. There are so many perfect lines in this novel, but one of my own favourites is 'the room looked like some old-age pensioner's last, lonely refuge': so sharp, so painful, and so clever because, in a story about the aching loneliness of the old, this is a description of young Cressy's attic idyll.

Yet despite, or perhaps because of, Elizabeth Taylor's understanding of heartache, this is also a genuinely funny novel, from Cressy's politely conversational 'I hear your husband left you', to the mystery of why birds' anxious pecking doesn't give them ulcers, or the 'good old days' when a maniac stabbed one of Harry's paintings with a penknife and made him, temporarily, a little more famous. No other writer interleaves pathos and humour with such brilliant, invisible skill, often in the same sentence: 'Oh God now *he's* ill, David thought angrily', or 'People are always coming here to collect for something – poppies and lifeboats and the cruelty to children'.

Taylor also understands better than most 'the terrible emotion of embarrassment'. So many of her characters suffer simply because they cannot bear to speak the truth, to admit that they are angry or alone. Her short story, 'Hester Lilly', contains the matchless, simple line: 'Deception enveloped them,' and all Taylor's novels are rich with ulterior motive, concealed longing, ham-fisted attempts to keep things running smoothly without snagging on emotion. The scene in which Cressy stands up to Harry Bretton is a masterpiece of painful parental love and artistic arrogance, perfectly balanced with the drunken witterings of the shabby family chaplain, who, trying ineffectually to dispel the storm clouds, keeps referring to a forgotten film. '"It was a good fillum," Father Daughtry said, spreading Ginger Rogers on the troubled waters.' With that one line, Elizabeth Taylor won my heart.

Father Daughtry, like all those of Taylor's characters who glimpse the abyss, tries to forget with alcohol: in enormous quantities. Her protagonists weave through the woods and cake-shops on a tide of whiskey, light ale and Quayne's vestal virgins' parsnip wine. When poor Cressy, horribly lonely, sniffs the antique dealers' hidden Cointreau and spills most of it on her dress, she thinks she has lost Paradise: 'I shall have to run away.' Instead she is rescued by David, because he feels sorry for her, and so begins the destruction of Midge's hopes and dreams.

Not Cressy's, though: to a girl raised on bean stews and Fairisle, the mere thought of Wimpy bars, launderettes and 'high-teas in depressing cinema cafés' is very heaven. Here, as in all her novels, Taylor writes so brilliantly about the muckiness of humanity: the way that our natural crudeness, our liking for a drink or private bad behaviour, seeps around the edges of our efforts to be sophisticated, from the barmaid who 'poked a finger into her piled-up hair and scratched secretly, pretending to be rearranging a pin' to Bretton's 'pearly-grey teeth' to the cleaner, Mrs Brindle, and her running commentary on life at Quayne: 'I must say my blood ran cold at one of the conversations I had no means of not over-hearing. The girl was crying – they're great for floods of tears up here … this was in the kitchen where they were having a bit of a tête-à-tête and taking not a blind bit of notice of me in the scullery. Clattering about with the dishes, I was, and coughing my head off.'

Taylor's matchless ear for dialogue, her eye for human ridiculousness, make her the mistress of the simile: a dog like an ant; a jaundiced baby like a blood orange; a man who seems to be overdoing his decline into old age, so that even his forehead resembles a bald wig. 'Cressy's room was like a stage-set for some depressing play about young-married strife, the very background for bickering and disillusion.' *The Wedding Group* is Margaret Drabble's *The Millstone* rewritten by Ruth Rendell, with other echoes too: Louis MacNiece's 'Hidden Ice', in its understanding of the rocks and currents which lurk under 'calm upholstering'; the bad housewifery and conjugal disappointments of Murdoch's Dora Greenfield in *The Bell*, who is the sort of woman men marry and then regret. However, what makes it entirely Taylor is the way that it combines their squalor and darkness with such wit and humanity and daring, so that one finishes it feeling exhilarated, expanded by compassion, like poor Midge whose heart has 'grown large with love'.

So what is to be Elizabeth Taylor's fate now? Will she sink slowly into obscurity again? Will she hover for a time at this new unsatisfactory level of semi-acclaim, fêted as a 'writers' writer', for the little that is worth? Or will she continue to rise? The author of *The Wedding Group*, *Angel*, *A View of the Harbour* surely deserves to be better known. It is in your hands. Forget her reputation: read her books. Then decide.

Charlotte Mendelson, 2010

PART ONE

CHAPTER ONE

The Quayne ladies, adjusting their mantillas, hurried across the courtyard to the chapel.

The three daughters of Harry Bretton – painter and pronouncer – had plain names which were impossible to shorten: Rose, Jane and Kate. At the time of the mass conversion – the whole family at once – to Roman Catholicism other Christian names had been added, but were not used.

The grand-daughters, two of whom followed them across the courtyard, had somehow lost their first names – Imogen, Cressida and Petronella were now Mo and Cressy and Pet.

Quayne was mostly a world of women.

At communal meals in the great barn, Harry Bretton presided, with the Chaplain, Father Daughtry, and Harry's wife, Rachel, at the other end of the long table, usually almost hidden behind an enormous tureen. He had no son. His daughter, Jane, had two – but the name was lost.

Cressy, this morning, watched them going into the chapel.

'I dare say I am abandoning my faith,' she had startled her mother by saying at breakfast one day.

'You "dare say"! What do you mean "you dare say"?'

Breakfasts at Quayne were taken in the daughters' separate houses, otherwise Cressy could not have made the remark. Her father, Joe MacPhail, did not raise his eyes from the newspaper; but her mother, Rose, put her cup back on its saucer with a shaky hand.

'One cannot *abandon* a faith,' she said at last, after staring first at Cressy and then, but without seeing anything, out of the window. The postman came bicycling up the path, right through her vision, but her brain did not take him in, and when something heavy fell through the letter-box, she started painfully.

Rose's father – Harry, the Patriarch – would take such behaviour as a personal insult, as if it were he whom Cressy was rejecting. There would be a Quayne rumpus, as there had been before, and Rachel, the grandmother, would get the worst of it, but none of them would escape entirely.

'Don't worry,' Cressy said coolly, irritated by her mother's expression. 'It never meant much to me. I shan't feel the lack. After all, you palmed it off on me without my being asked.'

Of all the girls, this one of Rose's had been the questionable one. The word 'recalcitrant' had been used on school reports. Her cousins had been so good and biddable, but – for Rose – there were always frightening interviews with Reverend Mother and, in the end, Cressy had not been allowed to finish her last year. Not exactly expelled, but the suggestion was that, all the same, it would be better if she did not remain. She had broken bounds, was often missing for hours at a time, and had had some strange notions, which younger girls were all too ready to listen to.

'You must talk to Father Daughtry,' was all that Rose could say now.

'He was only important when I *had* my religion,' Cressy said. 'Now he's no more than anyone else.'

4

This cloud had not yet broken, but it was building up to a great darkness, Cressy was thinking this morning, when they had all gone into the chapel, and the door was closed. Worse would follow. A dreadful fuss would follow. A great deal of talk. From some so much embarrassing and awful talk. From others, silences.

Would it not be easier, she wondered, to continue to go through the empty practices, for the sake of peace and quiet – since the religion meant nothing to her. At worst it could only be a waste of time and loss of self-respect. But she had wondered about this before, and decided no. She would rather – but only just – put up with the rumpus. The upshot of the ructions. That came in one of her father's Irish songs.

Whilst they were in the chapel, she wandered about the deserted courtyard, where hens pecked between the paving-stones. A Church of England charwoman, exempt from religious duties, was scrubbing the table in the barn, but she was the only sign of life.

Time always went slowly for Cressy, now that her school days were over. She had come home from the convent to nothing. To be a part of a busy, useful, self-sufficing community, her mother had said. This meant helping to bake bread, hoeing the kitchen garden, weaving dress lengths. The good life. Rejecting her religion was rejecting Quayne. The good life was the whole life. All parts hung together.

She would be expected to marry. Whom? Perhaps one of the young men who came to work in the studio with her grandfather. They would live pennilessly in one of the out-buildings (restored), and take their place at the long dining-table. She visualised it with the greatest of ease.

Leaning over the warm brick wall of her Aunt Jane's cottage, she picked an unripe fig. It was sheltered at Quayne. Peaches and nectarines grew well. Most years, grapes ripened on the south wall of the courtyard, against the studio, which Harry Bretton called the workshop.

The courtyard was large, had once been a rickyard. One side was the old farmhouse, the house of Harry, who had begun it all – the family growing into the community, with its religion and its way of life; all thought out by him, step after step, since the early days of his marriage, and his first successes as a painter.

The chapel, which they had built themselves of handmade bricks, was thinly white-washed, with windows of greenish wavery glass. In the farm cottages lived the daughters with their husbands.

The husbands were in no case of much account. As they had been acquired after the conversion, they were of the proper faith. Cressy's father was the Irish one. Gerald Fines, Kate's husband, worked at the B.B.C., and had to drive off to London very early most mornings, and returned home only just in time for eight o'clock supper in the evening – the great rallying point of the day, when they were entertained, over coffee, by a passage from Thomas Aquinas read by Harry who, even more than most people, loved the sound of his own voice. There was not, and never had been, any question of Gerald and Kate living somewhere nearer to London and more convenient to him.

Jane had married a Frenchman, Yves Brisson, who was a potter, and had a workshop in a clearing beyond the orchard, where he worked rather short hours. There was no proselyte amongst the husbands, who appeared at Quayne – sometimes a little too easy about religious matters. Joe especially, who would serve at the altar in slacks pulled over his pyjama trousers, for he found it difficult to get up in the mornings, and was always behind-hand.

There was also – from the husbands – a lack of reverence towards Father Daughtry, the Chaplain, who was ending his boozy days at Quayne. The two compatriots – he and Joe –

would sit in the village pub and, hazy with stout, talk of their Irish days. They were a great deal too much at the pub, thought Harry Bretton, who, at the end of a day's work, liked talk and music at home, where there was mead to drink, or cider, or his wife Rachel's elderflower wine.

The Father and Joe were both writing books, but neither of these works was likely to emerge for a long time, as their authors detested being alone in a room, without talk, for more than ten minutes, so that the necessary conditions for getting on with the job were seldom achieved.

Cressy loved and despised her father, and wondered how it could be possible to do both. Lolling against the wall in the sun, chewing the fig, she waited, as if doomed, for the others to come out of the chapel. I have a lot of my father in me, she thought. I only wish he had more of me in him. He had seeds of rebellion, but they came to nothing, choked by Quayne.

Here, at Quayne, everything was all of a piece; everyone, everything, fitted into the Master's scheme; for Harry Bretton had views on every aspect of life, and had, with what seemed to be the greatest luck, found that all formed part of the whole vision. Here, there was nothing he thought of as spurious, nothing meretricious, nothing counterfeit. All was wholesome, necessary, simple; therefore good and beautiful, too.

The outside world had jerry-built houses, plastic flowers, chemical fertilisers, materialism, and devitalised food. Beech woods on four sides protected Quayne.

It was to that world beyond the beech woods that Cressy was looking. She dreamed of Wimpy Bars and a young man with a sports car, of cheap and fashionable clothes that would fall apart before she tired of them. In that world she might find a place for herself. It was worth trying; for there was none here. She knew that she was about to become – if it had not happened already – the one flaw in the Way of Life – the first blemish upon

7

Quayne. Something which did not hold good, which ruined the argument.

Not only because of religion. One thing leads to another. Especially did so at Quayne. If one part of the concept was by the outside world seen to have failed, were not the others suspect? (Quayne, though cut off from the outside world, seemed curiously sensitive to its reactions.) So might not – for the sake of argument, not likelihood – Mo and Pet follow her own deviation? Coming to supper in shop dresses and plastic sandals, sighing for synthetic custards and tinned spaghetti. Then the world of Quayne might collapse, Rachel, in terror, trying to patch it up for Harry's sake, desperately ladling out the good soup – for the Quayne crises were very much mealtime events – and passing down bowls as fast as she was able. Cressy could imagine her poor grandmother.

From her place by the wall, she saw at last her cousins – Mo and Pet – come out of the chapel with their grandmother. They shook their long, blonde hair loose in the sunshine, and went off towards the kitchen, and their duties there. There was church for them – at one time or another – every day of their lives. And every day, too, mounds of potatoes to be scrubbed, or hay to be turned, sheets to be mended. (Cressy lumped church in with the other labours.) They knew nothing of the outside world, except for their school years at Chantoiseau in Sussex, and occasional holidays – mass holidays – in Wales. The company they had was one another. All three had been born within two years. The boy cousins were on holiday from Ampleforth, the school bills from there being paid by Harry.

They were now, the girls, quite isolated from the world. *Quayne Only* was on the signpost at the bottom of the hill, pointing up the rutted, leafy lane, down which water ran in torrents when there was a storm.

Harry came out of the chapel last, and stood for a moment

looking about him. The Master, one of his students had called him, and the family had taken it up, not unencouraged by him. At first they had used the name with a mingling of teasing and respect. It had stuck; until it seemed natural. He even thought of himself by the name, and now surveyed his world as someone of that title should. All that was done, and had been done, he thought with satisfaction, was to the glory of God, simply, reverently, and also by hand.

Cressy watched him with dislike, and she trembled a little.

He was a short man with a grey beard, rather long hair, thin on the crown, and protruding eyes. Always he wore a blue painting smock and sandals. He had hired a suit when he went to get his C.B.E., and he and Rachel – in clothes borrowed from her sister, a worldly woman – had looked very odd as they set out.

He came now slowly across the courtyard on his way to the workshop. Cressy made herself stay there by the wall, although she longed to dart away, and knew that she should be in the kitchen with her cousins. She had always feared and disliked her grandfather. When he came close to her, she stared into his brilliant blue eyes without blinking, waiting for the storm to break. He rested his hand on her head for a moment, as if she were ill, and then went on towards the barn.

CHAPTER TWO

'So many leaves,' Midge said. 'So many, many leaves.'

With a glass in her hand, she stood at the window looking at them.

Some sons may have a picture of their mother knitting by the fireside – but David's was of Midge with glass in hand, railing against something. The railing was hardly ever seriously meant. It was intended to interest, or amuse, or fill in a gap in the conversation, which was something Midge deplored.

This was a completely different world from Quayne, although David, at that moment, opened a letter from there.

'One is smothered,' his mother went on. 'Smothered and stifled by them. All dark green and black and dripping. I feel that they are growing out of my ears.' She was still on about the leaves. 'And so much grass! Your father always said that grass should be brown, if at all.'

Not that one took into account what *he* had said, she thought: but that little remark, which she had argued about at the time, had somehow stuck.

David, reading his letter, murmured something in reply to her, but the letter was so surprising that it held his attention.

'Dear Mr Little,

'Your article in the coloured supplement has caused me great concern.' The writing was childish and also backward-sloping. He read on, managing to get the sense of it, despite all the spelling faults. 'It was very wrong about me, and I feel I should explain this. To begin with, the photograph of me and the pig was really my cousin Petronella and the pig. Also, I am eighteen, not seventeen. And I have never called my grandfather the Master in all my life, and never would. Or call him anything.' (The last sentence had been scratched out.)

'It is unfair of you to accuse me of being religous without even asking me. As it happens, I make a point of not being, and at great cost to myself, if I may say so. And I only wear those sack-like dresses, as you so rudely call them, because I have no others, and I hate and curse them with all my heart every minute of the day.

'It is not our fault that we do not earn our livings and are oblidged to be maids-in-waiting – *your* description!!! But it is untrue to say that it is because we have never been educated, because we have, and can speak French for a start.

'More than anything in the world I would like to earn my living, and not remain here untill I am old. If you could ever find me a job, so that I could escape from this place it would ensure my everlasting grattitude, and my forgiveness for the injuries you have done me. This is a cry from the wilderness.

'With kind regards,
'Yours sincerely,
'Cressida MacPhail

'PS. I would do *anything*. Perferably something in your own line of country.'

Having remembered her husband's making his remark about the grass being brown, had silenced Midge for a minute or two, and David had been able to finish the letter in peace.

'You'd never believe it,' he said, and began to read it again, aloud.

When he had finished, he explained, 'It was that article I wrote about the loony-bin on Quayne Hill.'

'Those dreadful women,' his mother said.

'There's nothing like giving a good ticking-off before asking a favour. I like that. Poor little girl. She sounds at war with all the world.'

He went to find that coloured supplement to the paper he worked on, and when he brought it back, turned over the pages until he came to Petronella and the pig. Those girls had all looked much the same to him, and he had never been sure which one he had been talking to. All had pale faces and long, pale hair. Their brown feet, in clumsy, home-made sandals, were rough and scuffed. All bit their fingernails he noticed, and had thought 'no wonder'.

Communal luncheon was the subject of another photograph – all taken by his friend, Jack Ballard. The Master, sitting in a more impressive chair than the rest, had come out well, although his eyes and smock were a rather blurred and exaggerated blue. In fact, none of the colours was quite true, and the girls' hair had a greenish tinge. On the bare boards were loaves of dark bread, a casserole of beans, home-made cheese and flagons of cider. The faces were as plain as the food; but the young girls had a touching quality suggestive of another time in history – the turn of the century, or earlier. Girls were no longer like that, no longer even looked like that. On the white-washed brick wall behind the Master hung one of his paintings. It was of Christ, wearing an open-necked shirt and flannel trousers, carrying the cross, and followed by men on bicycles. In the background were factory chimneys and an English sky. The painting had come out quite clearly in the photograph.

'I wondered at the time,' Midge said. 'If that job wasn't rather too much on your own doorstep.'

She had just come back from the kitchen, and a delicious, steamy smell of mint followed her.

'Meeting them in the pub and so on,' she added.

She slopped some gin into her glass, adding vermouth in the same unheeding way. 'It will be another quarter of an hour,' she said, referring to dinner.

'It's only the Irish one – Joe MacPhail – of course, this one's father – that I meet in the pub, and only to pass the time of day. He kept well out of the way when I did the inter-view. All the others seemed to be lapping it up. Now this girl . . .'

'And the *priest* you meet,' his mother said.

'The Master lapped it up most. That awful meal. He harangued us all endlessly, about humility in art, humility in life. It's what he's got, he implied. No one else spoke, all the way down the table. Too humble, I suppose. They just went on eating beans; heard it all a thousand times before. Only the tame priest tried to put in a word or two, and then the Master took the chance to down some food, chewed and swallowed like mad, and then was at the ready again. Poor little girl,' he added, glancing back at the letter. '"French for a start." I like that. Who brought this, anyway?' He picked up the envelope which was unstamped.

'Mrs Brindle.'

Mrs Brindle, Quayne's Church of England charwoman (one of the true faith could not be come by), shared out her working mornings between Quayne and Midge Little. She brought a lot of interesting talk about Quayne to Midge, and would have liked to do vice versa, but Quayne was not interested in the Littles and their stereotyped and artificial world. Why she kept on there Mrs Brindle sometimes said she did not know, with that hill to push her bicycle up, and all the scrubbing when she got there.

'Mrs Brindle? Ah, yes, we have a go-between.'

'Will you answer the letter?'

'I'll apologise for mistaking her for her cousin. No one likes that – and especially as she's the prettier of the two. I can see that now. I'll post *my* letter, though.'

He was studying the photographs again – one, very Pre-Raphaelite, of the three girls gathering Madonna lilies for the chapel.

'I like that one,' Midge said. 'And the one of them all going *into* the chapel. It's like abroad.'

'The whole place was a treasure from my point of view.'

'It's come off better than anything you've ever done, I think.'

She walked about the room, sipping from her glass. She walked, she perched on the arms of chairs, she never flopped back on a sofa, as her son now had.

It was a beautiful room, mostly white and red, with bits of surprising pink and lime-green. Her husband had left all his books behind when he had run away, and they covered one long, red-papered wall, and gave richness and texture to the room, especially in firelight. This evening there was no fire, but even in the twilight of a dull summer evening, the interior of the room was not gloomy. It was a great feat on Midge's part that it was not. Outside, too close to inside, were all the leaves she had complained of, jasmine fringing the windows, dense lilac trees beyond. The garden was small, but there was a long, wide view of the woods, rising gently, blue, then grey, to the horizon. Somewhere up there, hidden, was Quayne.

David's hand kept dropping down and groping carefully for his glass which was on the floor. He began to compose in his mind a light-hearted, apologetic avuncular letter. He knew from a little – and not very recent – practice how to be an uncle. His mother did not seem to have learned how to be a grandmother. Her pink velvet trousers. 'For a start,' he thought.

He did not know that she dressed with the utmost care for his homecomings in the evenings. He imagined her always as she was now, had never – that he could remember – seen her otherwise. At breakfast, before he left, she was already ship-shape, never caught on the hop. An organised little woman. She looked her age, but in the smartest possible way.

All day, the evening was what she awaited. Dinner was organised, too. In the old days, before her husband went away and her other two sons had married, meals had been slap-dash, badly timed, some of the food nearly raw, other things over-done, especially meat, either too much salt or salt for-gotten. But he had no memory of those days. He thought of his home as one that had always run smoothly, revolving about him, where his friends came often, and liked to come, for Midge was a perfect hostess – mother, easy, undemanding. Kept young by her enthusiasms, ready to try everything, learn anything.

He knew that her two daughters-in-law did not like her. They seemed to be expecting her to harm them, to encroach, to monopolise their husbands. He was sure that she never would. But both lived so far away that the risk could scarcely arise.

He looked at his watch, feeling hungry. A quarter of an hour she had said, and a quarter of an hour it would be. From the kitchen through the open doors, came a smell of singeing meat, splutterings and sizzlings. Soon be ready, whatever it was. Smelt wonderful.

He considered his life with contentment, his appetite stimulated, juices running. Remaining at home, unmarried, might have been a problem to him. But if it had been a problem, he would not have done it, he told people who asked him if it were. To reveal to journalist friends in London that he lived in the country with his mother, usually caused a stir of surprise and disapproval. Apron-strings and umbilical cords came into the conversation. Even his brothers had urged him to set up house on his own until, amongst his many women friends, he decided on the one he would marry.

But the friends who came to the house understood the situation. And he fancied that some of the married ones – and most were married by now – occasionally envied him his life, with its series of light-hearted love-affairs, its lack of responsibility, the freedom to come and go as he wished.

His mother called him, on her way to the dining-room, with a dish in her hands.

As they sat down to dinner, he said, 'There's a girl – a woman – I'd like to bring down one week-end.' He could not get it into his head that he no longer had girl-friends, but women of his own age, who for some reason or another had not married. And even they were not so easy to come by nowadays. The cream had been skimmed off.

Midge appeared to welcome his suggestion, but had a rule that she must never ask him questions. Sometimes she took the rule much farther than was natural, or even polite.

'Nell Stapleforth,' he said, since his mother did not ask her name. 'She's to do with the advertising side of the women's page.'

'How interesting,' said Midge. She was always at the ready for these friends of his, on their side about everything from the start, woman to woman – often teasingly ranging herself with them against David.

She ate little herself, with pauses to watch *him* eating a great deal. This had been one of the pleasures of her life as a mother – his beautiful appetite, even in the days of the sketchy meals and all the failures. The other two boys had been such capricious eaters, finicking over kipper bones and cutting off fat, leaving the burnt frilled edges of fried eggs, and scorning her soufflés because they were tough and full of holes. David had eaten everything. With gusto. She liked that phrase. It summed him up, and she believed it summed herself up, too, in her approach to life.

'What did you have for lunch?' she asked. It was one question she could not resist and – if she had only known – one that irked him. To him, food was like sex, to be enjoyed, forgotten.

'Oh, just a beer and a bit of pie.'

She shook her head, as she always did.

'What about the week-end after next?' he asked, thinking back to Nell Stapleforth.

He was stripping the last bits of meat off a cutlet bone with his strong white teeth. He was the most handsome of her boys, she considered, and she loved to be told that he took after her, which he did not.

'Yes, of course. Any week-end would be perfect.'

'I must warn you that she hardly ever stops talking.' He dabbed his chin with his napkin and sighed contentedly. 'But she's what one might call a good sort.'

Midge was willing to give a welcome to all the good sorts in the world if it would make him happy. She smiled, and thought of menus and shopping-lists. Lately, she smiled to herself a great deal, for so many of his friends now were good sorts, plain girls with hearts of gold, on the shelf for all time, evidently.

Crême brulée followed the cutlets. She thought it was one of his favourites but, though he had two helpings, he had tired of it years ago.

After dinner, they sat for a little while in the drawing-room and then, as she had known he would, he looked at his watch.

'I might go down for a pint,' he said. 'Are you coming? I don't suppose you've been out all day.'

She had no friends. It had been a long time before he realised this about her, and he could not understand it.

'I went to the butcher's and to the post and had coffee at the Walnut Tree,' she said, trying to make much of her day. But she declined his invitation. She rationed her outings with him, wanting him to feel unfettered, dreading the words 'apron-strings' in his mind, or anybody else's. Two evenings ago she had accompanied him. Tomorrow, she might again.

As soon as he had left, the house seemed dull. She wished that she had gone with him, but knew that by bedtime she would be glad that she had not. But bedtime had to be come by, as all day long his coming home had to be waited for. Without him, she had no life – or only time to be spent perfecting what he would return to. Motherhood was now an art it had never been in the days when it was called for.

She washed up, emptied ash-trays, turned down his bed and drew the curtains. Then she walked about the drawing-room, a glass in hand again, and wondered about Nell Stapleforth, without anxiety.

Because it was August, which seemed to David the most banal month of them all, the trees were smothered in bitter, dark green foliage, the hedges bound over and choked by convolvulus and old man's beard and bryony. Down the lane from the house, nettles of the same darkness crowded up to the lower branches, and gnats danced above them.

But he was not as conscious of his surroundings as his mother was, and walked along quite happily to the pub. He was always pleased when he had her company, and pleased, too, when she stayed at home. She had the wit and the imagination to know this.

At the Three Horseshoes the evening had a familiar pattern – a few strangers listening apathetically to the regulars. The 'passing trade' sat on chairs round the walls, and the habitués stood about the bar, except for old Pitcher, a retired gamekeeper, who had his special place in the corner, and Joe MacPhail and Father Daughtry in theirs.

There were some middle-aged people giving Mother an evening out. Mother was dear, and the family took turns to lean across and shout at her. She looked a grumpy old party, David thought – aggressive hat, spectacles, fancy gloves – probably not much older than Midge, but those two were inhabitants of different worlds, members, almost, he felt, of a different sex.

Between old Pitcher and one of his cronies a long and exasperating argument was going on – about portsmouth reversibles and artillery bits, and other pieces of antique harness hanging about the bar. They were egged on by an American, who obviously thought he was discovering rural England at its most typical.

David leaned against the bar, talking to the landlord between customers, half-listening at other times to the tangle of conversation.

The American addressed old Pitcher as 'sir', with respect to his age, and Pitcher returned the compliment, with respect to the pint of beer he had been bought.

'All right, Mother?' shouted one of the family party, leaning forward.

Mother nodded glumly. In a slightly less shrill voice the daughter turned and said to one of the others, 'Mother's enjoying herself. She doesn't get out much these days. She's standing up to it nicely.'

Mother heard this and looked huffy.

'I was saying, you don't get out much, Mother.'

'I'm not deaf.'

The daughter sighed, and said in a low voice, 'You can never be sure with her.'

Joe MacPhail and the Father were on a reminiscent tour of the Dublin bars. As on other evenings, they were day-dreaming themselves from Davey Byrne's to the Bailey, stopping for a jar at the Russell. Would, no doubt, go on to Jury's and end up at the Hibernian.

They had looked up and nodded when David came in. That was all, for they kept to their own company.

Joe had looks that had been handsome, but had become pouchy and untidy. His mouth was puffy, sensitive. He rolled his own cigarettes with long, brown-stained fingers, and looked down at his glass of Guinness most of the time.

The Father was fat and moon-faced, with fuzzy patchy hair and odd bits of baldness. His fly-buttons were opened, and Mother was glaring at them contemptuously. Her daughter was trying to distract her attention.

'It makes a nice change, doesn't it, Mother, coming out?'

'No, thanks, you know I never have more than one. You must please yourself. Like you always do.'

'There's none so deaf as those as won't hear,' her daughter murmured sideways to her husband. 'It was a good idea of yours, Ken – dumping the old fridge in the woods. Got rid of that and made a nice outing of it.'

'I mind in the old days,' Pitcher was saying to the American. I mind this. I mind that. He was giving full value, now describing his late Lordship's pheasant shoots, year by year, gun by gun, brace by brace. He swirled round the last of his draught bitter and drank it swiftly, and the American, understanding the hint, took the empty glass back to the bar, paying well for his taste of village England.

'I was never for the Gresham,' said the Father. 'So brassy, so modern, and black with me own kind, don't you know.'

David kept looking towards the door, or out of the window at the car-park, hoping that one of his friends might come in.

'Blighty,' he thought. The darkness, the dull evening. Might up and hop it. There's all the rest of the world. He imagined Midge up and hopping it with him. She was quite game enough. Sometimes, England felt too small for him. For instance, he was physically cramped in this bar, and had to duck his head under the beams from which pewter pots hung, increasing the hazard. It wasn't only in this bar either. He remembered other places – Nell's mews flat, for instance, and, leaving Quayne that day, feeling smothered, wanting open spaces, and having, instead, to speed back to Fleet Street and shoulder his way amongst crowds, caught in a cleft between high buildings.

That visit to Quayne was in his mind again. What he had written about it was now all that he remembered; but since reading Cressy's letter, he had been trying to recall what else had happened. The day had been coloured by his dislike of Harry Bretton, and the success of the article had been mainly due to the asperity with which he had dealt with him. Readers who had always discounted his painting, had been delighted to discount the Master himself, and even those who admired his work had found a wicked glee in discovering the cracks in the idol so deftly revealed. David had heard later that the idol, in his vanity, had been delighted, too. He would have liked Joe MacPhail's opinion, but knew that he would not get it. He should have had the sense to talk more to the daughter, he thought. But the truth about her had come too late to be of use to him. It was all done with now. Quayne was behind him. There were other idols to topple; other Quaynes to be looked into.

'Ken thinks we ought to be making a move, Mother.'

David winked at the landlord and looked out of the window again. No one came, and there was a great to-do going on in the bar, the hoisting of Mother to her feet, offering her an arm which she pushed away. With another disgusted glance at Father Daughtry's gleaming fly-buttons she shuffled to the door, followed by her brood.

'Stable-door, old boy,' the landlord said, out of the side of his mouth, as he stooped over the Father to wipe an ash-tray. He stood close by while Father Daughtry fumbled hurriedly with his buttons.

David said good night and went out. It had been a tedious end to the evening. His mother had escaped it. But she was alone all day, and he ought to take her out, somewhere more exciting. He would do a bit of shouting at her when he got back. 'You don't get out much, Mother, do you?' Smiling to himself, he went home up the lane. It was dark now.

When he reached home, he went to Midge's room, as he always did, to say good night.

She was sitting up in bed, in a lace wrap, reading, and looking as if butter wouldn't melt in her mouth.

'Who was in the boozer, darling?'

He made it sound as dull as it had been, would have made it worse if he could. He was innocent of the workings of his own mind, and did not go into his motive for always belittling what he did without her, exaggerating the rain on holidays, the weariness of journeys, the tastelessness of food – everything that might make her glad to have stayed at home.

He told her about the deaf old party, and shouting back through the door 'Good night, mother,' went off to bed.

She was smiling, looking down at her book without reading. After a while, she closed it. She got up and took off her make-up and creamed her face carefully. Then she pinned up her hair and, when all this was done, she went to bed. She slept soon and peacefully, from a deep sense of security.

CHAPTER THREE

On the evening before Nell went down with him to the country, David visited his father. He felt guilty for not going to see him more often than he did, and tried to convince himself that the blame was on the other side, for it was his father who had defaulted and left them all in the lurch – not financially in the lurch, it was true; but his going had changed their lives, none the less. They – he and his brothers – had been in their teens, and had suddenly found themselves with their mother on their hands, instead of the other way round.

Archie Little had not left Midge for another woman. He had just left her. 'So *rude*!' she always said, seeing the funny side. 'I can't help seeing the funny side of it.' But the colour in her cheeks was from anger, not amusement. She had been badly shaken up at the time, incredulous, furious. Although spared jealousy, she was not spared something which seemed worse – the bare truth that he simply could not abide her any more, and had found a way of letting the world know it. He had expected his love to last, and it had lasted hardly any time at all, and he was not able to live with his disappointment. Discovering that he could not bear to live with her any longer, he had gone back where he had come from – to his Aunt Sylvie's home. He was twelve years older than Midge, and his marriage had made him seem more.

Her contempt had been corroding – especially as it came at a time when in the course of nature things were going wrong with him. He was losing his hair, and his joints were stiffening. The final crisis was having to have his teeth out: he was distressed by the idea of it, and felt that he was ageing fast. He wished that his wife need not know. During that time, she had been tirelessly cruel – had been sarcastic, had served food difficult for him to eat, had asked him never to leave the false teeth anywhere where she might catch a glimpse of them, as they gave her the horrors, she explained. She implied that he gave her the horrors, too.

He had seen her trying to make a fool of him before his sons, with his fuddy-duddy ways, his not being able to keep up to the minute or know the latest thing. He became very tired, trying to hide little aches and pains which beset him.

One day, he did not come home from his office. He telephoned from his club to give the reason. He was never coming home again, he said. Midge would not believe it. She became ill with anger, with waiting to tell him what she thought of him. She was obsessed by the thought of the scene she had been denied, and for weeks would pace about the house, or stand rigid, with closed eyes and moving lips. Several letters came, with business-like instructions about money. But he himself never came again. It was all over.

Since then, having taken up the old ways with Aunt Sylvie, he had not been happy. He had really been nothing and was glad of it – becoming a little more eccentric every year, a little more at peace, growing old fast. He had retired from business life but had by no means retired from work. Aunt Sylvie was difficult. She treated servants as she had treated them when she was young, so was usually without any; and both she and Archie had high standards to live by.

The house was on the outskirts of a town which had become a suburb of London, and traffic droned past it on the main road, and planes shrieked overhead. It stood in a ferny, dusty garden, full of old iris roots and broken terracotta path edgings. *Fernlea* it was called. The name was in curly gilt letters on the fanlight. Inside was a great darkness of mahogany. The sound of clocks ticking was softened by thick carpets and velvet hangings.

On this evening of David's visit, Archie had been in the kitchen, cleaning silver, and he led his son back along the passage, and sat down again at the table and went on with his job, wearing an apron over his velvet smoking-jacket. It was his evening for the finger-bowls and candelabra.

David sat down near by and watched him, knowing that it was no use offering to help, thinking that he would have sold the lot if it were his – the dreadful drudgery of it, and all so ugly.

'How is Aunt Sylvie?' he asked.

'Frail, very frail. Every day there seems to be less of her. One morning, I'll look in, and she'll have gone – nothing left.'

'Can't you get a nurse?'

'What on earth for? A nurse would be quite unnecessary. And, anyhow, she wouldn't hear of it. She gets about up there. She can take a bath. I fetch a chair and sit outside the bathroom door and chat to her, and she chats back, and then I know that she's all right.'

'It's not much of a life for you.'

'There's one's duty. One must do as much of it as one can. Apart from that, I'm fond of her. She brought me up from six years old. One has been cared for when one was helpless oneself, and now it is time for one to repay the debt.'

David thought of having to repay such a debt himself and was appalled. In the natural order of things, it would have been his mother's task to look after the poor old chap, when the time came. As this would not be, it seemed to him that he himself was in a bad position.

'Have you heard from Geoffrey or Edward?' he asked, thinking that it was just his brothers' luck to live so far away.

'I had a nice long letter from Edward. They took a trip to Melbourne. And very hot it was. A hundred and something.'

But David had heard of that letter before. It was way back – Christmas-time.

'And nothing from Geoffrey?'

'Nothing from Geoffrey,' his father said unwillingly. 'Not for some little time . . . let me see . . . oh, quite a little while it must be.'

Months and months, no doubt, David thought indignantly.

'How is your mother?' Archie asked, in a tone of great politeness.

'She is very lonely,' David said, staring accusingly at his father's busy hands.

Archie sighed, as if there were nothing to be done about Midge's loneliness. He looked resigned. 'She seems to have been in another life,' he said. 'I'm afraid I don't often think about her. Sometimes dream of her. It was all a sorry business. Aunt Sylvie was right. Don't you ever marry a woman so much younger than yourself. You'll only live to rue the day if you do.'

'I don't know any young girls nowadays – only ageing spinsters.'

'Well, take my word for it. She wasn't quite up to my weight, your mother. Aunt Sylvie said that from the start. "She's not up to your weight, Archie," she said. I remember her saying that.'

'What'd she mean?' David had an incongruous picture come into his mind, and tried to keep a straight face.

'Well . . . you know. Her father was in the hotel business.

Still is for all I know. Your grandfather, of course. Funny notion, that.'

He rambled on, working with an old toothbrush amongst the scrolled acanthus leaves of a candelabrum.

David hated sitting here in this depressing kitchen, listening to his mother being run down. It always happened thus. He looked about him, at the enormous dresser, at dish-covers and meat dishes of a size to conceal or carry twenty-five-pound turkeys, or sucking pigs, or haunches of venison. He wondered how long ago it was that they were last used.

'I only met him once or twice,' his father was saying. 'At the wedding of course. He was in his element then. You never saw so much champagne in all your life. It was just like a musical comedy, that do in the church. All those bridesmaids – only chosen for their looks, as you can imagine. Your cousin Ruth passed over because she had buck teeth. Of all the nonsense. And the hymns. "O Perfect Love", or some rot like that. Well, one soon saw what happened to *that*. "The Lord's My-hy Shepherd I'll not want,"' the black-smudged hand beat time to his wavering voice. '"God be in my head." Well, He never was, thank God. I have other things in my head. Of course, neither your aunt nor I has any religion. But in spite of it, the Vicar still calls. I used to think he had hopes of converting her – bringing her to God, don't they call it? But they must have gone by the board years ago. I think he just enjoys sharpening his wits on her. Your mother's managing all right on the money, is she?'

'I presume so.'

'What's she been up to lately? Does she still paint?'

'Paint?' It was an astonishing side to his mother he had never heard of before.

'Her face. And all that gin.'

'What do you mean "all that gin"?'

'Oh, she used to like her little tipple, you know.'

28

'Who doesn't?'

'I take your meaning. The decanter is in the usual place.'

'I don't mind if I do.'

His father sighed. The boy was picking up some of his mother's silly expressions.

In the dining-room, the table was elaborately laid for Archie's lonely dinner. More silver. More, too, on the shadowy sideboard, where the sherry decanter stood next to the tantalus, amongst biscuit-barrels and knife-boxes and epergnes. David poured out two glasses of sherry, and remembered to put them on a little silver tray.

His father had finished his polishing and was washing his hands.

'I never thought gin was quite the thing – a common sort of drink, like most of those who take it.'

Oh, Lord, he doesn't half go on, David thought, yawning.

Archie looked into the oven at some simmering mince, and then began to prepare Aunt Sylvie's tray, adding a plastic daffodil in a fluted vase.

'Such a good notion, don't you think? Nothing grows in the garden, except the Michaelmas-daisies later on, and the price of shop flowers is exorbitant. This came free, with the grocery order. It looks quite real, don't you think? I'm sorry, my boy, to be asking you to drink sherry in the kitchen.'

'What's the odds?'

Another of his mother's sayings.

'Smoking before dinner?' Archie smiled and shook his head reprovingly, as if he didn't know what the boy would get up to next. Taking the cigarette from a squashed old packet, too. Sordid.

'What happened to your silver case?'

'Nothing happened to it. It's at home.'

He must have driven Mother nearly mad, thought David.

'It's a long time to *my* dinner, anyhow,' he said.

'And when it comes it won't be worth eating, if I know anything.'

'I'm always telling you, Mother's a very good cook. Surely you haven't forgotten that.'

'Well, we won't have an argument about it. You're the one who's got to eat the stuff. I will only say that in my day she couldn't even boil a kettle.'

He cut some faded-looking grapes off a bunch and put them in a dish on the tray with one of the newly-cleaned finger-bowls.

'I shall have to go,' David said, finishing his sherry.

'It's been very good of you to look in. I do greatly appreciate that. Please don't bother to wash the glass. I'm glad to say that Mrs Whatshername will be here in the morning. She deigns to give us an hour or two on Fridays.'

'Shall I carry up Aunt Sylvie's tray?'

'No, she will expect me to do that.'

He could not say that Aunt Sylvie would not be pleased to see 'that hussy's boy'. David's brief visits to her room raked up all her old grievances about his marriage to Midge.

'I haven't made the sippets yet,' he added. He glanced at the clock, and then fetched a loaf from the larder.

'Well, I'll just nip up and say "Hallo".'

'I shouldn't if I were you, dear boy. It's her Italian day, and you know how rigid she is. And yours is so poor.'

'Non-existent.'

'Well – then . . .'

On Mondays, his father and Aunt Sylvie spoke only in French to one another; on Thursdays, in Italian – to keep their tongues in, although David could not think for what. And why those particular days, he had not asked.

'O.K., then. I'll be dropping in again soon. Is that all you're having, mince and toast?'

'It's ample for our ageing digestions,' his father said. He had a nice, gentle smile, David thought, regarding him as the stranger he was.

As he drove homewards, he suffered the by now familiar sensations of shame and pity and irritation. He was always relieved to escape from that house, where the old clocks ticked, the old hearts beat. He felt protective towards his father and was annoyed that he should do. Everything about Archie had been irksome, whether in the family or out of it, and especially in his way of leaving it; and he was amazed that his mother, easy-going though she was, could have borne his behaviour for sixteen or something years.

When he reached home, he found her in an especially gay mood. 'All that gin,' he thought, refusing some. 'I've been drinking sherry,' he said.

'Oh.' This was all the comment she allowed herself, and it was after a hesitation. She knew where he had been, but would not refer to it. None the less, she let her gaiety underline the contrast between here and *there*, and dinner was especially delicious.

So she could not even boil a kettle! David thought. His father's memories were clouded by injustice. As he ate, he thought of the little dish of mince amongst all those giant tureens and ladles and silver-plated covers; and, after the mince, those two pecking at a few grapes, like sad old birds.

CHAPTER FOUR

Cressy's first steps towards freedom had not taken her very far from Quayne – only down the hill and into the village, making the reverse journey of Mrs Brindle's.

It was Mrs Brindle, in whom she often confided, who had found her the job at the antique shop on the Green. It was one she had been offered herself, but had been unable to take because of what she called 'the poor remuneration'. In the village, she acted as a free employment bureau, always being able to place someone, or oblige someone else, knowing who could spare an hour or two, or sweep a chimney, or mend a teapot.

The village was on a main road between London and the sea, and was dominated by motorists, the passing trade. With its black and white cottages and hollyhocks, the trim Green and the pond, its partly Saxon church, it was a place to run out to, or pause at – for tea at the Walnut Tree café, a drink at the Three Horseshoes, to stretch cramped legs with a little amble past the shops, all bright with paint and swinging baskets of geraniums and wrought-iron signs.

The antique shop was rather more austere than the rest –

white-painted, bow-fronted, with the name *Moorhead* in plain black letters above the window.

If David had been disposed to, he could have found the job for Cressy even before Mrs Brindle did; for the Moorheads were his friends. But Cressy's future had been something he would not meddle in. He had written his deft little letter of apology to her, and ignored her plea for help. She had decided to make her own way and had angrily tried to put him out of her mind, hoping, she told herself, that she would never see him again.

Yet, at the end of her first day at work, she did. She was at the back of the shop, polishing brass, when he walked in with Nell Stapleforth. 'Well, well,' he said, raising his eyebrows, and went through to the room at the back to have a word with his friends, leaving Nell to potter about the shop as she had wanted to.

Toby and Alexia Moorhead were brother and sister. Their father had been the local Rector. When he died, he had left them a little money, and they had started their antique shop. It had solved for them the problem of finding some kind of work which they could do together, and both had a flair for buying and had made a good business of it. They were a quiet pair, and self-contained, with a physical beauty which seemed the reason for their never separating, never being seen with inferior partners. Both were tall, and had silky black hair, and a gesture of putting it aside from their brows. They had dark skins and rather long, fine features. They looked like twins, but were not; though of a near age, in their late twenties. This morning of David's visit, they were wearing the same putty-coloured shirts and trousers.

'What on earth is *she* doing here?' David asked. 'It *is* that MacPhail girl from Quayne, isn't it?'

'She's cleaning a coal-scuttle, I hope,' Toby said.

'You know, I wouldn't wonder if she isn't quite a bothersome and eccentric girl.'

33

'Hush,' Alexia said, going on with her accounts.

All the same, Cressy, sullenly polishing the scuttle beyond the half-opened door, had heard him.

'Charming!' Nell kept saying to her, taking up, and putting down, and peering short-sightedly at porcelain marks and price tickets. She had a little dog like an ant on a silk-cord lead. It was hardly a dog at all, and made her seem even larger by the absurd contrast.

Cressy, wondering who she was, felt spiteful towards her, and would not have minded if she had dropped something and broken it, or if her dog had lifted its leg against the needlework-covered stool.

'Enchanting!' Nell said. 'Enchanting!' she said again, louder, as David came back into the shop with his friends. She held up a Wedgwood bridal group, and Alexia stood rigid until it was safely back on its shelf. 'Yes, it's one of our favourite things,' she said, when she could breathe again.

'So you've managed to get out into the wide world?' David said to Cressy. The 'wide world' being just the village, she thought his words must be sarcastic. He was wondering how it could be any better sitting there in her dark corner amongst the polishing rags than up at Quayne feeding the hens, or whatever it was she so resented doing there.

To his dismay, he saw, before she bent her head, that her eyes had brimmed over. A tear actually fell on her dirty fingers. He dared not now introduce Nell to her, as he did to the others, or make any more inquiries, or even glance at her again. He simply seemed to include her in the general farewells, but not in the hope of meeting again that evening.

'She is very sensitive,' Toby said.

'Touchy,' said Alexia.

'But willing.'

34

'In a driven sort of way.'

'And cheap.'

It was after dinner, in the red and white sitting-room, with a little fire, just lit, to brighten things up, as Midge had said.

They were discussing Cressy.

'She *is* inclined to cry,' Toby explained to David. 'Don't worry about it.'

'One simply *can't* worry over touchy people,' Alexia said. 'One would spend one's life . . .'

Midge was usually in her element when she was contentedly, quietly pouring out coffee after a good dinner, listening to the young people talking; but, this evening, something was different – nothing deeply wrong, only the surface pattern of such occasions a little changed. She could not lay a finger on it, and was trying to, feeling abstracted, as she filled the cups and handed them to David.

'Now sit back, Ma; you've done enough,' he said, taking his own cup.

There were renewed praises for her cooking.

Of course, she reflected, the young people themselves were getting older. Nell, for instance, was almost like one of her own generation. Midge thought her so ungainly, although she carried herself well – like a caryatid, though with nothing more to support than the weight of all her auburn hair. Once in a chair, she slumped and sprawled, her skirt caught up above her fat legs, showing stretched stocking-tops, suspenders, edges of tatty lace. She had kicked her shoes off, and kept feeling about for them with her toes. Her ringed fingers combed through, puffed up her fringe. Older men, on the newspaper, thought her a 'fine woman', David had told his mother, finding it rather amusing.

Perhaps, Midge thought, it was Nell, with her careless, slovenly ways, who had ruffled the evening. She had decided last night, on her arrival, that she would easily be able to get on with her. If David could find something in her, she would assiduously search for it herself.

There had been footsteps in the night, across the landing, a door softly closing. It was not her business, she decided. She had tried to go to sleep, willing her mind to other lines of thought, yet waiting all the time to hear the noise of the lavatory being flushed, and the footsteps returning. Nothing had happened, but a long, long silence, and she had fallen asleep while it still continued. 'Under my roof!' she had thought, on first waking in the morning. Then she had smiled, realising that the phrase sounded more like Archie's than her own. At the back of her mind, so *far* back that she hardly knew it was there, was the idea that extramarital relations might make the other sort unnecessary.

They had finished talking about Cressy, and Nell was reading David's palm, leaning forward over the dog on her lap, his hand in hers. She found all kinds of conflicting traits, the most broken heart-line she had ever set her eyes on, with a chain of islands; recklessness; fickleness: but in the end she could see, with perhaps a little stretch of imagination, calmer days ahead, and a child – certainly one child.

He listened mockingly and, as soon as he could, withdrew his hand.

Now it was Alexia's turn. She held up her palm obligingly, but with her eyes fixed on Nell's face, as if it were *her* character which was under scrutiny.

'This couldn't be more straightforward,' Nell said. 'There are just the four long, clear lines – life, head, heart and fortune. Great honesty and forthrightness.' She turned Alexia's hand about, folding the fingers, and uncurling them. 'The girdle of Venus is the only unusual thing – very deeply marked with indentations.' She ran a finger along it.

'That's where I cut my hand on some broken glass and had to have three stitches,' Alexia said.

Nell returned the hand and sat back in her chair, stroking the dog. 'It's all crap, anyhow,' she said.

'Oh, please do mine!' Midge begged.

'My dear, it's only a joke. My mother once said to me when I was young, "Just learn to make good coffee and tell fortunes, and you'll never be at a loss." She tried to make me smoke, too. Just one of the little social graces, she explained. Something to do with one's hands, you know.'

As she was now using her hands to rake through her hair, and dandruff was falling, Midge thought that her mother had had a point.

'Please!' she implored, offering her palm.

'What month were you born in?'

'July. Cancer. That dreadful word.'

'So you scuttle sideways?'

'Not Mother,' David said.

'All right,' said Nell. 'Although it's only nonsense. Let's see how many bits of broken glass may have changed *your* fortunes.' She spoke in a low, amused voice, and groped again for her shoes.

Toby and Alexia swept their hair from their foreheads and leaned forward.

She's beautiful, David thought, looking at Alexia. She was something he had never dared; but he liked to have a little future daring in his mind.

Midge sat like a little beggar-girl on the rug before Nell, with her hand held up beseechingly. It was a thin hand, wrinkled and shiny, with dark, raised veins.

It would be more wicked, David thought, still watching Alexia's intent face, really much more wicked than stealing another man's wife.

'The life-line,' began Nell, with Midge listening like a child, 'is long, but broken. However, there are parallel lines protecting those breaks, reserves, I think, from strength of will.' Midge blushed with pleasure. 'From the head-line I see single-mindedness rather than deep intellectual powers. You see, you must forgive me; I speak as I find.'

'And, as you explained, it's all crap, anyway,' David said.

Midge only murmured encouragement.

'You are home-loving. The heart-line is unswerving. There is a deep concern for those you love, amounting to possessiveness, really.'

'Oh, come off it, Nell,' David said. 'You go too far with your silly game.'

'No, no!' said Midge, trying to silence him. 'Let Nell say what she thinks. After all, you're the only one now that I have to be possessive *about*, so you are the only one who can know. I'm not in a position to judge.

'Three children,' Nell said, folding Midge's little finger. 'You see – one, two, three.' She pointed to some creases.

'You knew that already,' David said.

I knew it all already, Nell thought. She looked away from the hand, at the fire. 'Under the influence of the moon,' she said, 'so a woman of moods.'

'David. Am I moody?'

'No,' he said. 'Who would like some brandy?' He got up. Only his mother said 'yes'.

'Moody's not necessarily derogatory,' said Nell. 'As I was saying the other day to a friend, it depends on the *predominant* mood. If that's a dark one, it comes as a relief to have a change.'

David thought, you didn't say that the other day to a friend. You're saying it now to my mother. Who is your hostess?

'Home-loving, Nell?' he asked, attempting to get off danger-ous ground. 'Well, that's true, isn't it?' He looked inquiringly at Midge, setting down the glass of brandy on the table by her chair.

'I suppose I love it,' Midge said, looking round the room. 'Though sometimes, I can't wait to get out of it.' The evening before, for instance, when they – David and Nell – had gone off after dinner, without asking her to go, too. It was so unlike him, she had thought, pacing about the room after they had gone. Nell had made him behave out of character. If they had been going simply for a drink, she could easily have been invited, and would probably have refused. They had obviously driven up to Quayne Woods or somewhere of the kind, and made love in the car. So uncomfortable but, she supposed, many young people's first experience of sex these days.

All this talk of 'home-loving' had annoyed her. They were trying to turn her into a *Hausfrau*, and the talk had gone back to praises of her cooking.

'Well, you can hardly see *poulet à l'estragon* written deeply on my hand,' she said, rather hastening over the French words.

Now she was impatient, and drew her hand away. She sat down again, and began to sip her brandy, feeling that Nell had been deliberately rude. And she was disappointed. There had been nothing about her courage, or sensitivity, or artistic leanings, or high romance, or her sense of humour. Especially, 'artistic leanings' and 'a sense of humour' she had hoped for and expected.

'I myself loathe cooking,' Nell said, leaning back again, and settling her dog in comfort. 'To me, it's like having a migraine. And all the fuss and nonsense that's written about it. I read it on our women's page. There was one last week about pastry baskets filled with cherries. "Make angelica handles if desired," it finished up with. Who on earth could desire an angelica handle?'

'I sometimes envy you career women,' Midge said, looking from Nell to Alexia and back again.

'Anyone can get a job,' Nell said.

She had come for this week-end, wondering if she wanted to marry David, and if she could get her way if she did. She had made up her mind that she would not be sad, however it turned out, feeling sure that true love was something gone by: she had not been successful at it, and hesitated to run the risk again. But David or no, she decided she was not taking on Midge.

At Quayne, that Saturday evening, after beans and bacon, there were stewed windfalls, and a reading from D. H. Lawrence. This was followed by coffee and a monologue. Lawrence had set Harry Bretton off on one of his favourite tacks, and the discourse this evening – with no embarrassment at all to himself – was on the role of woman in the life of man.

Dabbing his lips with the red and white navvy's kerchief tucked under his beard, he examined, with an attempted ruefulness, the nature of his own sex.

He had an extra stimulus to talk this evening – his friend, Leofric Welland, who was staying in the house. Leofric had written one book about Harry's works, and had another in mind – and some of it on paper – about his life. Harry knew this was in his mind and liked to help build up the picture. He had even offered him a plot on which to build a house in the orchard, so that he could always be at close quarters, but Leofric's wife had had enough of Quayne from time to time, and would no longer spend even a week-end there. Many different excuses had to be made.

'In spite of all our grand ideas,' Harry was telling him, 'we are only perverse children at heart. If we have the intellect, it's our women who have the wisdom. No one knows that better than one's wife.' He smiled at Rachel, and she smiled back. 'One's mate,' he amended. 'For all our precious ideals, our inventiveness, it's the essential, instinctive mother-wife we crave at last.

We return, after our escapades or great deeds, to *her*, for forgiveness and healing and approval.'

Rachel tried to look forgiving and healing and admiring, but had an abstracted air.

He just makes me want to vomit, Cressy thought. Her mother, aunts, cousins were conditioned into acquiescence. Pet went quietly round the table, refilling coffee-cups over people's shoulders. Mo kept pressing a finger into crumbs on the table and licking them. Joe MacPhail folded his arms across his chest and thought how he had wasted his life.

'It is to that instinct we call and return.'

Leofric, who had been thinking for some time of leaving his wife, noted the words none the less, and hoped to remember them.

Unfortunately, Father Daughtry, who disliked this sort of talk, had drunk too much Guinness before supper, and was inclined to chatter about other things, trying to keep himself awake.

'Did you never see that fillum of Ginger Rogers, now? What was the name of it?' he asked Cressy, who had never heard of Ginger Rogers. He asked Gerald Fines, who glanced nervously at Harry, and then said, in a low tone, that he had no idea.

'Ah, what was the name of it. I have it on the tip of me tongue. That was the best fillum I saw at any time.'

The cinema was a great pleasure of this last part of his life, and often he spent dozy afternoons there, on into the early evening when, before he caught the bus back from Market Harbury, he could have a jar or two at the Crown, where he had cronies.

'In England,' he said, 'there's nowhere to sleep but at the fillums. A man could make a fortune setting up some nice little dormitories, cubicles, don't you know, where you could have a lie down for a shilling or two when you came over weary.'

His glance wavered towards Harry, and away, having met the expression of kindly patience with which he waited for the interruption to cease.

He's a good simple soul, Cressy thought. He must feel all at sea at Quayne. She was wearing her new dress, of chemically-dyed, machine-woven cheap material. She, too, had been to Market Harbury.

Her grandfather continued – in a not louder, but more distinct voice, his dissertation on the weakness of man; but he spoke of this weakness with both pleasure and arrogance. Woman, the haven to which the explorer returned, he treated of with reverence, for God had created her to this purpose.

'It's one-way traffic,' Cressy suddenly said aloud, not having known that she was going to.

Her father, Joe, was thinking along the same lines, but only fitfully. Father Daughtry, having turned his mind for the moment from Ginger Rogers, had let the words 'airy guff' come into it. He glanced at Cressy in astonishment.

So the storm which had been building up for weeks was about to break. The upshot of the ructions. And at a meal-time, too; and in the presence of Leofric Welland. Cressy's meek cousins looked down at the table. Her mother and aunts looked towards Harry. Yves and Gerald and her father looked at her.

Before Harry could speak, Cressy, burning her boats, said, 'You think nothing of women. You won't even let us vote at elections,' she added frantically.

Feminism was to Harry an ungainly aberration. 'What a lark!' he always said – that women should have a vote, above all want one. Then he would go on to tell them how to use it.

Now, he said evenly, 'The law of this sad old country refuses you the vote. Not I.'

'I'm speaking as a woman,' Cressy stammered, and her

cousins giggled, and then were suddenly quiet, feeling all about their bent heads, looks of reproval.

'Cressy!' Rose said imploringly.

'Come, Cressy!' her father said gently and pushed back his chair and got up.

'It was a good fillum,' Father Daughtry said, spreading Ginger Rogers on the troubled waters. 'Only the name escapes me.'

Tears came to Cressy's eyes, and she stood up, too, clumsily, with her face turned aside.

'Don't distress yourself, child,' Harry said in a clear, low voice. 'We have all been young, and know what a business it is growing up. I'm sure there is no one in this room who has not kicked against the pricks at some time, and understands the misery of it.'

Cressy, at the door, turned round bravely and let them see her brimming eyes. 'I don't suppose there's any collection of people in the world who've done it less,' she said.

Joe had his hand on the wrought-iron latch. He clicked it up quickly and took Cressy out into the moonlit courtyard.

Leofric Welland retired early that night, but not to go to bed. Various people about that courtyard could see his lighted window for a long time.

Harry went for a stroll and, coming back across the orchard, saw it, too.

CHAPTER FIVE

'Poor little Cressy! She can't sing in tune with us any longer,' Harry Bretton had said, when she had left the barn with her father. He had smiled with especial fondness at his two grandsons, Bartholomew and James, sitting at the other end of the table, on either side of their grandmother. Rebellion from schoolboys might have been more easily expected, he thought. But these two came and went, and revealed nothing. They led mysterious lives. They had just returned from staying with school friends – a good Catholic family, no doubt; but, all at once, it seemed to Harry that they were too much away from home. And in formative years.

Pet and Mo, always singing beautifully in tune with Quayne, were made to see Cressy in a harsh and ugly light – her distorted face, her clumsy rage and, now, her discordant voice. They had mixed feelings about her new dress.

Rose had wondered whether to get up and go after her husband and daughter. She hesitated, till she had left it too late, and remained where she was.

When at last she went over to the cottage, Cressy had gone to bed, and Joe had spread out his writing things on the table, and was trying to get to grips with his book. He always turned to it when troubled by guilt and loss of self-respect.

'Whatever has come over her?' Rose asked in a peevish voice. 'After all that Father's done for her.'

'She's a perfectly normal girl. It's we who are abnormal.'

'Don't let *us* have a quarrel.'

'No, of course not.'

'All this having to have a job. Serving in a shop! Well, there's one thing, *that* won't last very long. But you should have put your foot down.'

In bed, Cressy was, in her misery, longing for the shop. She dreaded the next day, and cursed it for being Sunday. She would feel as if they had hung a bell round her neck to warn her cousins of her approach.

Last night, Leofric Welland's presence had no doubt saved her from an angry storm, but that would at least have cleared the air which she could imagine would be full now of wary amazement and sickening forgiveness.

She had not been far wrong, for the only sharp words next day were from her mother, and they were sharp indeed. She was blamed for ingratitude, for callow behaviour, for drawing attention to herself. The list reached much farther back than anything to do with last night's contretemps; it touched on her wilfulness of many years, and the old troubles as a schoolgirl. A deep antagonism had grown between Rose and Cressy.

'You are only shirty because you don't get enough sex,' Cressy said, in her coolest, most goading voice.

Rose was too staggered to do anything but gasp 'How dare you!' – which enabled Cressy to continue.

'You're all edgy, and it's just because you're afraid of having more children. "We aren't meant to think of the sexual act separated from fertility." The times I've heard that. So this house should be full of children. Or else you daren't *have* sex, and so you're edgy, as I said.'

'You are only a child. How can you understand what you're saying?'

'I understand that you don't believe in birth-control; you've only had me; and you're edgy.'

'There are other ways . . .'

'And I can see you're too embarrassed to discuss them. And so should I be. But I don't want to know.'

'Those are private matters. One day, when you're married . . .'

'Don't worry. I won't be having that sort of husband, and I won't be that sort of wife.'

'I don't know what you mean,' Rose said, turning aside with a look of distaste. Standing there by the window, drooping, her head half-averted, she might have been posing for one of her father's pictures, as she so often had. Her skin looked pale against her peacock-blue dress, which was stitched with green and held against her breast with one of Yves Brisson's pottery ornaments on a leather thong. She never wore make-up, and her hair was braided round her head.

She was not tearful, like her daughter, and never had been. In fact, she had had – apart from Cressy – so little to cry about. Her girlhood had been unclouded. Because her life at Quayne had been so right for her, she blamed herself, and not Quayne, that her daughter was at variance with it. She herself had been so contented. Her father had found for her, and kept for her, a beloved husband. She had never been parted from those she loved.

'We will say no more,' she said curtly, seeing Joe coming up the path.

During these quarrels, Cressy felt stimulated. She triumphed in shocking her mother, who seemed so much less articulate,

made defensive, relying on worn old phrases, whereas she herself was carried away from safety on a tide of words.

Afterwards, she was unhappy, and she knew that the quarrels
had their ill-effects upon her father, whom she loved and pitied.
Laziness had allowed him to give up his life, and strength had
gone out of him, and she knew it, and guessed that, from time
to time, he suffered.

'You have a wicked little head on those young shoulders,'
Rose said, at the end of one angry scene. Those words had
stayed, and echoed, of all the words her mother had ever said.
They frightened her.

Apart from Rose's attitude, there was everybody else's.

Her grandfather was tender towards her – modelling himself
on the Good Shepherd, she thought. Leofric Welland, who had
prolonged his stay, thinking that interesting events might take
place, at last departed, disappointed.

Her cousins she saw little. It was like school all over again,
with the goody-goody girls warned off her.

Her father who, these last few days, was working on his book
as never before, was sorry for her, but could do nothing. It was
a hopeless relationship, the one pitying the other. Lately, she
had begun to appear pitiable. She had a sad and distracted air.
Her shop dress was new no longer, and looked as if it were a
punishment inflicted on her; buttons had dropped off and been
lost, and seams had come undone and frayed. She could not
afford another.

She was grateful that Father Daughtry behaved to her as if
nothing had happened. He had only a hazy idea of what had
been said on that Saturday evening, and he liked the girl. Her
nervy faith was being put to the test, and she needed peace and
quiet. It was the worst that could happen to any mortal, and so
many voices must confuse her.

'Oh, I am sick at heart,' Cressy told Mrs Brindle, as they met on Quayne Hill, going in different directions to work. 'If it weren't for my job, I'd die.'

'I'll have a word. I'll see what can be arranged. You leave it to me,' Mrs Brindle had told Cressy, meeting her another time, dragging her way wearily up the hill from work on her half-day. She hated her half-day.

It was wonderful to Cressy to have someone say that to her. Although she feared nothing could be done to help her, the words themselves were a comfort.

She could not go on all her life – or even very much longer – with things as they were at home, with every mealtime an occasion to dread. Her sense of isolation was terrible.

Mrs Brindle was well known as a tower of strength. She knew it, and the knowledge spurred her on to greater efforts. 'I can usually find a way round things,' she said. She had said it when her husband died; when her son-in-law fell out of work, and the girl next door got into trouble. She had said it all through the war.

'It's hell up there for the poor girl,' she told Alexia, who had shut the shop, but had been seen pottering within, by Mrs Brindle, who had propped up her bicycle and peered through the window. Alexia had unlocked the door. She was alone. Toby had gone to the other side of the country to a sale, and she was impatient for his return, longing to hear about his day, and to see what he had bought.

'I just called in to see how she was getting on,' Mrs Brindle said. 'Five guineas!' she cried, looking at a brass oil-lamp. 'Oh, dear! Oh, dear! I threw all ours away when we went on to electricity. That makes me want to kick myself.'

Alexia smiled patiently.

'No, I looked in,' Mrs Brindle went on, 'feeling a bit responsible, naturally, really having been instrumental in getting her placed with you. I wouldn't like to think I've done the wrong thing by either you or her.'

'We're pleased with her. I hope she's pleased with us. She tries hard – if only she wouldn't leave the cleaning things about.' Alexia picked up a rag from a chair. 'But I wouldn't say anything. I'd rather go round afterwards. And if only she didn't cry so much. I'm afraid customers may think we're cruel to her.'

'Customers *wouldn't* think that. One glance at you and Mr Moorhead would suffice. They would surmise that she had private troubles, which is the fact of the matter.'

'Otherwise, she's so willing . . .'

'She's a good girl, worth double those others, with their niminy-piminy ways. Butter wouldn't melt, etcetera, etcetera. She's the only one of that bunch I've any time for. Barring that poor old priest. He's always been very pleasant, apart from his dirty habits. *Personal* habits, I should say.'

Alexia wondered what other kind of habits could be dirty.

'It's as clear as daylight to me what's going on up there – call it witch-hunt, or what you will. Poor girl! No, what I meant to say was he drops his food down his front – a nasty eater. Egg-stains, the lot. You name it, he's got it. But he's good at heart. It's nice to meet a religious man like that. Of course, your father,' she said hastily, '*he* was out of this world. One in a hundred. A saintly man. He was a byword, and that goes without saying. I'm sure I never heard one thing said against him at any time, and believe you me I get about this village, and have for more years than I care to think about.'

Alexia believed her. I wonder what she's really come about, she thought.

'But that poor old sod up there,' Mrs Brindle went on, 'although he's not in the same class as your dear father, and never could be, all the same he wouldn't harm a fly. It restores your faith in human nature, doesn't it? Maybe there's a bit too much of this' – she lifted her bent elbow – 'but who's to cast the first stone, after all? I always say that, I say, "Who's to cast the first stone?"'

'I sometimes say that too,' Alexia remarked gravely.

Mrs Brindle swept on. 'Sometimes he quite confides in me, knowing it won't go any further. "Mrs Brindle," he said the other day. "I'm a terrified old man this morning." Some Monsignor was coming to lunch. "Monsignor" – is that the right word? I'm C. of E. myself, like you. He said, "There'll be such intellectual arguments, I won't dare to open my poor bloody mouth for fear of showing my ignorance. They speak French, you know," he said. It emerged that he can't. That's the only time they buy shop wine at Quayne. It seems the Monsignors or what-have-you only drink claret. He enjoys that, but it makes him nod off. "They look down on me, Mrs Brindle," he said. "They smell the turf on my poor old hands." Where he comes from, they call peat that, you know. Just for the moment, I thought he was talking about his horse-racing. "They masticate their little ideas," he said, "and I'm left out in the cold – my proper place." "Proper place!" I said. I was beginning to boil. Yes, I can tell you, I was really beginning to boil.' She seemed to rise up, and then simmer down. 'He's so human,' she said, 'You can't help liking him.' She glanced again, thoughtfully, at the brass oil-lamp, and then added, 'No, if you had some little attic. It wouldn't matter how small. I know it would seem like heaven to her.'

CHAPTER SIX

David and his friend Jack Ballard, the photographer, had had their success with the series on living painters, and now were sent off to explore the literary shrines of England – a rather duller assignment, they considered.

Midge was at this time living in the future, as she lived most of her life, and the present, with David away, went very slowly for her. He came home only at week-ends, and the days between formed a pattern of slowly rising spirits from the despair of Monday onwards.

David and Jack Ballard went motoring up and down England in search of the scenes of its past glories – to Rye, to Dorchester, to Haworth and Chawton. August was out, and leaves beginning to fall. There was now a more interesting light for photography. A fine blue mist hung over Haworth, and Rye was bathed in gentle sunlight.

Midge tried to pass the time. There was no cooking to do, no meals to plan. She lunched on bread and cheese and gin-and-French, and supped off shop cakes and sherry. She cut off the dead roses, and hoped for a last crop later on, she made new curtains for David's bedroom, and went to London several times about her winter clothes. It was all work for the future.

The evenings were terrible to her, for it grew dark earlier each day. She paced the sitting-room, found that she talked to herself, switched all the upstairs lights on at dusk, in readiness for going to bed, and all night long imagined burglars breaking in. David, enjoying himself, sent postcards. She wished that there were a literary shrine near by, but there was only the village lady-novelist, and she was of no account.

Mrs Brindle alone brightened Midge's days. They worked together, for company, turning out rooms, and talking about Quayne. Midge had an almost childish interest in the long serial story Mrs Brindle so willingly unfolded. She even called at the antique shop, on the pretext of a hunt for opaque glass. She introduced herself to Cressy, had a chat with Toby and Alexia, lingered, admired the Wedgwood wedding group, and left empty-handed.

She often saw Harry Bretton about the village, in his long smock and the chef's cotton over-trousers he always wore. His carved shepherd's-crook had been brought by a disciple from Delphi, and from the same place he had a shepherd's hooded cloak for winter. It was snug, but smelly, and people coming up in the train with him from London would sometimes move from his compartment into another at the first opportunity – especially in wet weather. Midge saw him one morning, as she came out of the Walnut Tree café. It was soon after her meeting with Cressy. She knew who he was, but she and her box of cakes meant nothing to him.

'I'm leaving Quayne. I came to say good-bye,' Cressy told her grandfather.

He had been warned by Rose, and was ready for this interview, and Cressy did not take him by surprise, as she had hoped.

Apart from the thought of the outside world and its comments, he was greatly relieved. The girl spread confusion, like a poltergeist.

'It will always be waiting for you, when you want to come back – if the outside world, as I believe you call it, doesn't come up to expectations – which it may not,' he added gently, sorrowfully.

He was in his workshop. On an easel was a half-done painting of 'The Marriage at Cana'.

He had been sitting humbly before it, perched on a stool, looking at it through narrowed eyes, when Cressy entered. She, standing beside him, looked at it with wide-opened eyes, and thought that Christ had a distinct look of Harry about Him. She also thought that the bride and bridegroom, in stylised modern dress, resembled the figures in the Wedgwood wedding group in the antique shop – the one which both Nell and Midge had admired so much, and which she herself thought crude and pawky, like some fair-stall ornament.

'Well, you won't be very far from home,' Harry said, still deliberately staring at his painting, and speaking as if he had more important matters on his mind. 'And' – he turned then, and smiled – 'it will save your poor little legs all that going up and down the hill. I know how you young people like to save your legs.'

He was in an exceptionally good mood, because the next day he was off on one of his walking-tours in the New Forest with Leofric Welland, his most willing listener. Fifteen or twenty miles a day, he thought complacently. At my age.

'God will be with you, little Cressida,' he said, dismissing her. He stood up, put his hands on her shoulders and his beard against her forehead. 'You won't make your mother and father unhappier, I hope, by not coming to see them very often.'

'No,' she promised.

So much drama, and the arguments with her mother, and her father's silence, had left her very tired. She felt that her head was full of tears, but for once they did not fall.

Harry sat down on the stool again and tried to turn his thoughts to a study of his day's work. Without their looking at one another again, the farewell-scene was over.

A little later that day, Joe went down the hill with Cressy, carrying her suit-case. They talked brightly, but with almost numbed lips.

It's such a little way away, he kept reminding himself, shifting the case from one sore hand to the other. But it wasn't where she was going; it was the reason for it, that haunted him. Other daughters of her age went off – to their flats in London, even to foreign places, but did not leave such bitter wreckage behind them. And Rose on her own he had to return to.

Thinking of this, he said, 'We'll leave your case at the shop, and then why not us have a little drink together at the Horseshoes? I don't believe I've ever taken you out on your own in all my life.'

'Oh, I should love it,' she said, and her lips became less numb, stretched by her smile. 'I shan't know what to ask for. Can I have wine, like the Monsignors?'

'No, I'm afraid wine's out at the Horseshoes.' He smiled, too. 'It's a very modest establishment.'

'Sherry, then?'

'Sherry,' he agreed.

With his free hand he raked through his pockets. From long experience he could tell copper from silver by touch.

They walked on down the hill quite jauntily, thinking of the future and its possibilities.

In asking for an attic, Mrs Brindle had known what she was about. The lay-out of the rooms above the shop was perfectly clear in her mind, from her having worked there for a previous owner.

And she had said it would be heaven, and it was.

'I shall be so happy here,' Cressy said, dumping her suitcase down, and rubbing her hands on her skirt.

Alexia looked at her in astonishment. The room, to her, seemed hardly fit for human habitation. They had never redecorated it, and the uneven walls were papered with a powdery, faded pattern of roses. It smelt fusty, and its one window looked on to a blank wall of the Three Horseshoes.

To Cressy, it seemed beautiful, as the place where her new life would begin. On the little bare landing at the top of her own flight of stairs was a gas-ring and a wooden shelf, a saucepan, a kettle, and a plate or two: for one of the conditions of her being there was that she should not encroach upon the Moorheads' evenings. They liked to be alone together, cooking their supper, listening to music and, later, going over the accounts or the catalogues of auction sales.

'I'll leave you to settle in,' Alexia said, having explained about the gas-ring and the electric-fire and apologised for drawers sticking and floorboards creaking.

'And this first evening, if you want to borrow some eggs . . .'

'It's very kind of you, but I bought a tin of beans. As a matter of fact, I'll unpack later. My father came down with me, and he's waiting next door at the Three Horseshoes.'

'You should have brought him in,' Alexia said vaguely, thinking that the girl was starting off well by not having done so.

'He never goes in anywhere, except the pub,' Cressy said, following her down the stairs. 'I suppose he's rather retiring.'

That suited Alexia.

From below came the sound of a Dave Brubeck record, and a smell of olive-oil being heated, then, above the music, there was suddenly a great spluttering as something was slipped into the pan at the right moment. Toby was cooking the supper.

'You've got your back-door key?' Alexia asked. 'We have to be very careful about locking-up here, as you can imagine.' She opened the door of the sitting-room office and watched Cressy going out into the cobbled yard at the back of the shop, where they kept pieces of statuary and urns and wrought-iron garden furniture.

Although she was sorry for the girl, she wondered if she was going to be a nuisance. She had had a happy girlhood herself and, spurred on by Mrs Brindle, had over-imagined the miseries of Cressy's. All the same, what she and Toby wanted and hoped for was to live their lives together, and in peace.

That evening seemed one of the worst of all to Midge. She could not nudge away thoughts of the future – those thoughts that so often spoiled the present. She wondered about old age, when her life might be like this all the time, with no hope, as now, of David's returning – his last postcard was from the Crabbe country – either tomorrow, the next day, or any other day.

The silence frightened her. This evening, nothing moved, except for an occasional leaf floating down through the heavy air. The garden, with its mauve and yellow autumn flowers, was perfectly still, growing dark.

She had been working there until dusk and, as she came across the lawn to go indoors, the windows faced her, black and blind.

The house, a Georgian cottage, had been added to, years ago, by Archie. He had built on the big room, and other rooms above it, in white clapboard, with a slate roof. It had been skilfully done: it was a success, and she loved it. Only herself in it alone dismayed her. She remembered the house when it had been quite full, and noisy and untidy. She was remembering it now, going towards it. At this hour, she would have been bringing in off the lawn all the things the boys would have left there at their bedtime – rugs and cushions, cricket-bats and dirty beakers. Then, when she had gathered everything up and dumped it in the hall, she would cook some scratch meal for Archie, feeling tired and irritated, but surely happier than now, and certainly not frightened.

Inside, she washed her hands, still thinking of the old days, looking at her set face in the glass above the basin. She locked the door, switched on a great many lights, poured out a drink. Then she went back to make sure that she had locked the door, began her usual pacing about, and kept glancing at the clock.

If David married, she would have to leave it all – sell up and perhaps go to live in a flat in London, for company and protection. And then what would she do all day? And where could all her lovely things go in a flat – the old furniture and the modern pictures – the pleasing blend of Archie's family things and what she herself had collected?

Or she could stay on here and take in a paying-guest, whose purpose would be to lessen her sense of isolation. She had thought it out so many times – one solution after another; but none was a true solution. 'I don't *want* a lodger,' she murmured aloud. Her heart added, I simply want David here – David and his friends, all the young people. But the young people seemed to be ageing faster than herself. The present could not last for ever.

The telephone ringing so unexpectedly in the quiet house startled her. She almost ran into the hall to answer it, then, finding that it was a wrong number, she came back slowly. She took up her glass and sipped, her heart still beating fast, and her mouth drooping as if she might cry. Cruel, she thought. How awfully cruel. But cruel of whom she did not know.

That had certainly made the silence worse – the silence when she stopped going about the room, clicking her heels on the parquet floor. She could bear it no longer, she thought, and decided to drive somewhere, anywhere, simply not to be here. It was so far off bedtime, and going to bed, in any case, she dreaded.

She unlocked the garage, backed down the drive and went out into the dark lane. There were no lights, no houses, until she reached the village – only her headlights combing through the trunks of trees on either side.

The last bus stood empty by the Green, brightly lit, reflected in the pond. She drove slowly. Even the sight of that had lifted her spirits. In the cottages were other lights – sometimes only the blue-white illumination of a television screen in a room whose curtains were undrawn. Against golden blinds were silhouettes – of a shrouded birdcage, or a geranium in a pot. A faint glimmer shone through the antique shop from the room behind. The Three Horseshoes was the most lit up of all – the sign flood-lighted, and brightness streaming through the chintzy windows. She drew up the car and went in, feeling a little apprehensive and self-conscious, for she had never been there without David.

The bar was not very crowded. It had a murmurous glumness about it, in spite of the barmaid – whom Midge had never seen before – dazzling in a lurex-woven dress. The landlord introduced her to Midge as Gloria.

'Oh, I know your son,' she said. 'There's quite a likeness. I expect you're often told that.'

In fact, Midge was not told it nearly often enough, but always warmed up when she was.

Gloria brought a look of London to the bar, and old Mr Pitcher glared crossly at her. When she bent down to reach for a light ale from the bottom shelf, she showed a sun-burned cleavage. Her hair, of a uniformly butter-colour, was built up high with a false piece of nylon. Midge was 'dear' to her from the outset.

'G. and T.,' she repeated, when Midge gave her order. 'Ice and lemon, dear?'

Midge poured most of the tonic water into the glass. She had had nothing to eat, and was nervous about driving home. That was another thing, she thought. She liked to be taken out, not to have to fend for herself. She sat down by the bar, on one of the high stools, so that she could chat to the landlord and not seem solitary.

After a while, when she had lit her cigarette and settled herself, she looked round her. In a corner, the girl, Cressy, was sitting with her father. She had been staring at Midge, and smiled quickly when she caught her eye. She looked flushed and shabby, and at once began to make random conversation with her father.

Other conversations, from other parts of the bar, mixed and became a tangle in Midge's head. There was a couple behind her, sitting at a table, drinking, very slowly, lager and lime. The young man's hair was long; the girl's short.

'We ought to go and see my rich old aunt at Worthing,' he said. 'Considering I'm the only one she's got to leave her money to. Not that you'll see much evidence of it. She's as mean as sin.'

'All the better for you,' the girl said.

'I mean if you can put up with that awful house for half an hour. Show willing, you know.'

The girl listened intently, her hand on the table. He put a finger against one of hers, and kept it there in a proprietary way. They stared at one another, as if hypnotised.

'Well, Mother, you're getting quite giddy in your old age,' said a loud and sycophantic voice.

Midge half-turned her head, as if hearing an echo.

'I've got a rich aunt, too,' the girl behind Midge said. Looking backwards, Midge saw the two fingers tapping about one another, lively and playful, as if with a life of their own, nothing to do with the conversation, or the long and penetrating looks.

'Really rich?'

'Well so-so.'

'Anybody else but you?'

'Nobody.'

There was a contented pause. Then, 'How old?' he asked in a low voice.

'Thirty-nine.'

This information seemed to cause no stir of disappointment.

'Married?'

'No.'

'Lesbian?'

'I s'pose so.'

'Don't you, Mother?' the other woman was shouting. 'I said you like the Horseshoes, I said.' Lowering her voice, she added, to the man beside her, 'It makes a nice change for her. Poor old thing. And we've all got to get old one day.'

As I was telling myself earlier, Midge thought grimly, glancing at Mother, who was buttoned up tightly in navy serge. Poor old thing indeed. Growing deaf, carted about for her treat and having it rubbed in all the time. No wonder she looked so furious.

David shouting at *me* in a pub one day, Midge thought. Taking me for *my* treat, and everyone saying how good and patient he is.

'She's taken quite a fancy to coming here,' the indefatigable daughter was saying. Her husband was mute, staring into the smoke-haze.

Midge listened with interest. They were just as David had

described them to her one night on his return from the pub, and now she was trying to remember every word that was said, so that she would have something to tell him when he came home from the Crabbe country.

'Enjoying your drink, Mother? It goes down well, doesn't it, after a hard day? She had all her washing out before nine,' she said, turning to her husband. 'Just look at her ankles, Ken. We could hardly get her shoes laced up.'

Ken did as he was told, but without much show of interest.

They were so awful, so very, very awful, Midge thought. But they weren't funny, after all.

'This is awfully nice,' Joe said. 'What I've missed, taking you out!'

In truth, he was finding it rather a strain, being cast together with her on their own. He realised that he had scarcely ever had a conversation with her before, and could think of little to say. He knew nothing about her, in fact, and was much too gauche to know how to find out. 'But still,' he added, smiling, 'after all, you were hardly old enough.'

'Not old enough? Oh, really! When you think what any other girl of my age would have done.' But he wouldn't have any idea, she decided.

'I dare say. But girls grow up slowly at Quayne. Not a bad thing, you know.' He added the last sentence from loyalty to Rose. Poor Rose – so stunned these days from the threat that what she thought of as her 'whole' vision of life, was really incomplete, as Joe had guessed all such visions must be.

'Have you been away at all?' the barmaid asked Midge. It was her stock question at this time of the year.

'Nothing exciting. I went to stay with my father in Buxton. Lovely country all round, of course.'

'So I hear,' the young woman said vaguely, as she lifted ash-trays and glasses, wiping underneath them.

The visit to Buxton had been while David was in Rome with Jack Ballard. Her father, a widower now, had taken her round his haunts, driving the second-hand Bentley. A tour of the constituency, he said. Even she had found the pace fast and the routine boring. And she disdained to be seen with his entourage, those hard drinkers he had gathered round him in his retirement – men in belted, camel-hair coats, with trilby hats pulled forward over purple faces. They entered pubs in a gang, her father, Good Old Bertie, going ahead to buy the first round of doubles. Bertie Reynolds and his Outriders, Midge had once overheard them called. Each year, on her visit, the Outriders were fewer. There were so many funerals amongst them, wonderful send-offs, by all accounts, with the drinking-sessions immediately following them beginning in an air of exalted grief and then, through reminiscence – 'Poor old Jack would have wished it this way' – becoming more boisterous than usual.

'And you?' Midge asked the barmaid in her turn. 'Have you been away?'

The sunburned cleavage had been acquired in Spain, it seemed.

Cressy, feeling rather muzzy, looked at Midge with great admiration. She wondered how much just such a soft, pale coat would cost. And such soft, pale shoes to match. She would have liked her to join them, but guessed that she was probably the very sort of woman her father could not bear.

'I think we must be off,' Joe said. 'Your mother will wonder what has happened.'

Rose, he knew, would not wonder for one moment. but he had only a shilling left. Two sixpences. No mistake about them, hiding in the corner of his pocket.

'Drink up, Mother.'

Mother took a gulp of brown ale, leaving a pale froth on

her upper lip. Her daughter whispered in her ear and Mother, straightening her hat crossly, touched her mouth with her glove. 'She's as pleased as Punch,' her daughter said to Ken. 'You couldn't have done better if you'd given her ten pounds.'

Trying endlessly, but without luck, to keep everybody happy, had given the daughter a discontented look. Her cheerfulness had a snappy edge to it, and one day, Midge decided, deaf or not, she would look like Mother. Not very gruntled, to say the least.

'Good-bye,' Cressy said shyly, on her way to the door. She, too, had been pleased by her outing. David had not come; but on some other evening he might. And she was going back to her baked beans and her new life, and she felt elated now, and – whether it was the sherry or not she did not know – was no longer tearful. She would creep in through the back door and up the stairs, and go softly about between bedroom and landing, and be no trouble at all. They would not know that she was there.

The young couple had at last finished their lager and lime and had, with hands entwined, departed, and, next, Mother was hoisted up on to her poor old feet. Good nights were said; but not by her. She had become wary of saying anything, rarely having managed to hear what had gone before.

'Well, let's all have a drink,' Midge said in a reckless tone, when they had gone. Without knowing, she was an echo of her father.

It was cosy and quiet – she and the landlord and the barmaid gathered together, and relaxed. She made up her mind to come more often on her lonely evenings.

'That coat makes me green with envy,' said the barmaid, woman-to-woman. 'Here's how!' She took a sip of Guinness daintily. 'That's more like it.' She poked a finger into her piled-up hair and scratched secretly, pretending to be re-arranging a pin. 'And how's that handsome son of yours?' she asked.

'Long time, no see,' the landlord said.

Driving home after the bright lights of the bar was a different matter, and Midge regretted her outing, thinking of the empty house ahead, and wondered if, after all, she would ever make a habit of it.

As she was shutting the garage doors, she heard the tele-phone ringing. She ran across the gravel sweep, pushed the key into the lock with impatient hands, and almost fell into the hall. As soon as she did, the ringing stopped.

Frustrated and trembling, she stood still and listened. The silence had a terrible finality. She was, at first, afraid to disturb it, and when at last she could move, she took off her shoes and went quietly across the hall and up the stairs.

The two telephone-calls now seemed menacing – both the wrong number, and this unanswered one. She thought of bur-glars trying to find out if the house were unoccupied, or if a man's voice replied.

She stood in her room, shivering, and chafing her hands, imagining men with nylon stockings pulled over their faces for masks, breaking windows and climbing over the sills, or forcing locks. There would be no need for them to gag her or tie her up, or knock her into unconsciousness, for, long before they could, her heart would have stopped from fright.

She undressed and from habit took off her make-up, creamed her face, and pinned up her hair. While she was doing this, she had a sudden idea. She collected together her gold bracelet, her pearls, her diamond brooch, some ear-rings, and her mother's sapphire engagement-ring. She put them all into a polythene bag and dropped them over the banisters into the middle of the hall floor. Perhaps – she hoped – that might satisfy any house-breakers, and save them the trouble of searching any further. Before she lay down, she pulled the telephone on to the bed beside her and, with all the lights on, closed her eyes and waited for sleep.

There were the usual night-noises about the house – creak-ings, sudden explosions and whirrings from the refrigerator, a rose-twig scratching on a window-pane. She tried to analyse each sound. Something dropped heavily in the garden; perhaps an apple, perhaps not. In the end, worn-out, she slept.

She was wakened by a downstairs door being quietly closed. It was the front door, she knew, from the sticking sound of its draught-proofing strips. Steps crossed the hall, and paused. The bag of jewellery was no doubt being examined. She laid her hand on the telephone, but was afraid to lift it, and let anyone hear her voice. And could the village policeman, a mile and a half away, help her now, or should she dial 999 and wait for a car to come from the town? Her heart-beat was like the sound of heavy boots lurching uncertainly through snow. The foot-steps began again, were on the stairs. Without hope, she snatched up the receiver, tried to dial, tried to scream.

David opened the bedroom door and stood there, with the bag of jewellery in his hand. She slumped forward, dropping the receiver, covering her face, and began to weep – wonderful steady tears of relief and exhaustion.

When she was able, lifting her wet, creamed face to him, she tried to explain. He wore Archie's bewildered frown, but not, happily, the look of distaste which had usually gone with it. He had never known his mother disorganised, his memory did not reach back so far. The shiny face, the hair pinned up, made her look old and, at the same time, piteously young.

He laid down the jewellery on the dressing-table with horror. It gave a clue to premeditation, to a long fearfulness endured, the terror she had striven to combat. He was filled with embarrassment and consternation and – that trembling hand on the telephone – with guilt.

'I'm sorry,' he said several times, punctuating her incoherent tale of terror. 'I didn't know. I simply didn't think,' he went on. 'I tried to telephone, but I rang off quite soon, thinking you must be asleep.'

'I feel so foolish,' she cried. 'A grown woman. It's so absurd.'

'Are you always scared of burglars when I'm away?' he asked gravely.

'Only at night. One seems so isolated here.'

He frowned again. The burden of it.

'Well, I'm home now,' he said, matter-of-factly, and smiled.

He knew that her possessions – her 'nice things', as she called them – were most precious to her, and yet they had been put out as an offering, a sacrifice, in the hall, a ransom for the taking. That was the proof of her alarm.

He said, 'Jack had to go back early by train. I tried one or two hotels on the way home, but they were full, and then it was too late.'

She wiped away tears on the hem of the sheet, like an unhappy little girl.

'Are you all right now?'

She nodded. 'Only ashamed of myself,' she said.

'For heaven's sake, don't be.'

He came to the bed and kissed her forehead. It was clammy to his lips, and he felt repelled. She flinched away.

'You don't want this now,' he said, putting the telephone back on its table.

His voice was anxious, yet optimistic, as if he were visiting her in hospital, and she lay back peacefully against the pillows and closed her eyes.

CHAPTER SEVEN

'One of our worst mistakes,' Toby said to David. 'Even worse than that carriage-table that had wood-worm.'

'*You* bought that,' Alexia reminded him. 'This mistake is *mine*.'

They were in the sitting-room office behind the shop, and David kept glancing towards the half-opened door.

'It's all right. She's gone to the pub with her father,' Toby said. 'Every Friday evening they meet there. She gets quite excited about it.'

'Poor child!' David said.

'Exactly!' Alexia agreed. 'This is the trouble. One evening, the silence up aloft was so . . . so . . . I was conscious of her up there keeping quiet. I said to Toby that we simply must ask her down – just for once, to show . . . I ran up and tapped on her door, and do you know what she was doing?'

'No,' David said, with interest.

'She was leaning out of the window, staring at that brick wall of the Horseshoes.'

'Did she come down?'

'Yes. She asked us questions for half an hour, and then looked at the clock, and said she must go to bed.'

'What sort of questions?'

'Had we loved our parents; did we ever go to dances; were we religious; how much did my sweater cost; did we hope to be buried or cremated . . .'

'Both so delightful,' Toby said.

'And things like, was everything in the shop insured, in case she should happen to break something; and what does vodka taste like, and have we ever stayed at the Ritz. You name it, she asked it, as Mrs Brindle would say.'

'Well, I am rather interested in the answers, too,' David said, 'but I dare say you've had enough of it. Doesn't she ever go home?'

'Yes, between services on Sundays.'

'To have such a waif on one's hands,' Toby said.

'It's the feeling of guilt hanging over us,' his sister said.

With feelings of guilt David could sympathise. 'I'll take her out one of these evenings,' he offered.

On Sunday afternoons, Cressy trudged up Quayne Hill, through the cluttering leaves, breathing in the smell of moss and mould. She lived amongst the smell of old things – old stuffs and furniture in the shop, the damp wallpaper in her bedroom. And when she reached Quayne, there was the scent of rotting apples, and incense, and Rachel's wines fermenting.

Joe MacPhail was usually dozing, with a newspaper on his lap; but one Sunday, she found him sitting at the table, writing his book. He had decided that steps must be taken about his own despair, and his daughter's dissatisfactions. It had been a comfort to him to realise and it was the first time he had truly realised it – the importance of money. It was something he could work for, aim at, something practical to do. The old torments of sloth, of procrastination, of accidie (a word much used by his father-in-law) had been no goad like this immediate one of wanting to take Cressy to some of the places he had briefly known as a young man. Romano's, he knew, no longer existed, and he had come upon it in its decline; but were there not still Rules and Boulestin's? He imagined Cressy settling back on a red velvet banquette, while he casually flipped open the padded leather wine-list. Once, he had known a thing or two about wine – from the old days at Jammet's in Dublin with his father, who had also known a thing or two. Cressy would try to conceal her respect and astonishment at this new side to him, wearing a careless air, as if on every evening of their lives they dined in such splendour. But when the wine-waiter had reverently with-drawn, she would smile at Joe, bright with excitement and complicity. Both would be dressed in a way that Rose would abhor; but Rose was not there. He always skipped that part of the day-dream, and went on to wonder what had become of that dark suit he once had had. Though it would be no good for nowadays. Cressy would realise – from seeing young men in the Three Horseshoes – that the trouser-legs were far too wide, with flapping turn-ups. He would have to buy a new one. There would have to be a very good advance on his book. Money, he suddenly saw, was the answer to almost everything. Mr Burns and Mr Oates would have to cough up a great deal, or he would want to know the reason why. After all, the book had taken years to write.

It was also a satisfaction to be discovered by Cressy, with his papers all over the table, and his fingers black from the drib-bling dip-in pen. He was wearing his tweed jacket, made by Rose from unwashed sheep's wool. It was creased, but stiff. The oil in it kept the rain out, and it was still faintly beaded with moisture, from his just having collected kindling-wood in the drizzle.

Rose was in the kitchen, making a sponge cake for tea. She was always strung-up when Cressy came – waiting and waiting for her – and then finding that they were strangers. So she – as Joe – liked to be busy with practical things. It would be too absurd to sit by the fire and entertain her daughter in conversation.

When she saw Cressy coming up the path between the brussels sprouts, she was as apprehensive as ever. Each week, she expected her to give in, to ask to come home; but it never happened. Always in the early evening, Cressy said good-bye, and thanked her mother for tea, as any visitor would. And then what did she do? Rose wondered. Get up to? But Cressy did not say.

Rose was folding egg-whites into the mixture when Cressy came in. At least she still walked in through the back door, and did not go round and knock at the front.

'How've you been getting on?' Rose asked, without looking up, for she was at the tricky stage with the cake-making, and might have timed it with a stop-watch for this very moment. I am embarrassed with my daughter, she thought, and she felt great envy for her sisters, with their happy, Quayne existences. She tried to sound bright and welcoming, but her face had settled to a wounded look. She always wore it now.

Cressy tried to think of little bits of news.

'You look peaky,' Rose said, sighing. She loved this devious child, but the love seemed to be all worry and sadness.

'I'm all right.'

'What did you have for lunch?'

'Oh, the usual – roast beef and things. Apple tart.'

Her mother did not know that Toby and Alexia were not providing nourishing meals. She had never met 'those two', as she thought of them, and hoped she never would. She almost felt that they had kidnapped her only child. She seldom went down to the village.

Joe called out, and Cressy found him in the living-room, sitting at the table, grinning like a schoolboy, his papers spread out before him, and piles of what he euphemistically called his reference books. Although he was getting his book out of other books, there was, just the same, a lot of hard work involved.

Cressy stood by the window, looking out across the orchard. With its rough, hoary grass, it was a disheartening sight. Leaves drifted down in the misty air. Under the trees, her Pre-Raphaelite cousins were picking up windfalls, like girls in a legend, searching for hidden treasure. Cressy, nowadays, liked to keep out of their way. Although in their very latest teens, they still looked at her uneasily – the obedient children who had been warned off a bad influence.

She could smell the sponge-cake baking, and longed to be eating it. She lived on things on toast, and not enough of them. Her mother came in and put another gnarled branch on the fire, which kept giving out soft puffs of smoke. Logs dribbled on to the bed of ashes that had accumulated since the beginning of autumn.

Joe decided to make a pretence of going on working. He, less than Rose even, wanted Cressy to be there as a visitor. He flopped open a heavy book and began to turn its pages. Dear Lord, he thought, I used to know more than I know now. My poor old brains have drained away.

'How's Father Daughtry?' Cressy asked, for something to say. These Sunday afternoons were tedious and exacting.

'Why?' asked her mother, looking up hopefully from the fire.

'I only wondered.'

Rose bent down again and rearranged the branch. 'He's the same,' she said.

At last it was teatime, and the sponge-cake was put on the table, with a loaf of Rachel's bread and a pat of Rose's butter. The books were cleared away to one end.

As Rose was pouring out the tea, Harry Bretton looked in on his way back from the compost-heap, which was his favourite leisure occupation. He sat down at the table, with his chair at an angle, as if he did not intend to stay long.

'You're pale, my child,' he told Cressy. 'Our poor little shop-girl. Rather Dickensian. You should be out of doors more.'

'My work is indoors,' she said. She had tried with her parents, but could not help being sullen with him.

'Do you still think it is a good idea?' he asked gravely.

'Yes.'

'You're not simply being obstinate?'

'No.'

Harry had loved his children tenderly when they were little, and still did. He could not bear to see Rose's unhappy frown, and she could not bear to hide it.

'Is it worth it?' he went on, taking a piece of sponge-cake.

'Worth what?'

'Making your mother anxious.'

Cressy looked surprised. 'Angry', perhaps: 'anxious' had not occurred to her. She had thought she had weighed everything up, had exchanged Quayne for hunger and loneliness and insecurity. The very sight of her grandfather had made her glad she had done so. Now Rose's anxiety was thrown upon the scales and with it her own callousness.

However, depressed as she was, she was still hungry. The cake was so fresh, so light and eggy, with a slight flavour of orange-peel.

The logs dribbled; the conversation languished. Harry took another piece of cake, and praised it. Joe took another slice, too, and Cressy watched them. There was always plenty of home-made cake about for them, she thought crossly; but not for her.

'There is no need for anyone to be anxious,' she said. 'I'm nearly nineteen years old. Other girls of my age can go to Timbuctoo without their mothers getting into a fuss.'

'I just wondered if you were truly happy – as we know your cousins are truly happy – or punishing yourself and others for the sake of rebellion.'

'How can working in a shop be rebellion?' Cressy asked. And, damn it, if he wasn't helping himself to a third slice, and she had hardly begun her second.

'Now, Cressy!' Joe said softly. 'No point in going over old ground.'

For a moment, Harry fancied that this might be intended to rebuke him – but discarded the idea. At least he was sure he had his daughters' generation in hand.

'Well, Rose,' he said, 'she appreciates your cooking, if nothing else.' He smiled. The red lips parted above the beard, showing pearly-grey teeth. He handed the plate to Cressy and she took the last slice.

That evening, she was more disconsolate than ever, trying to knit herself a sweater, which kept going wrong. She had never been gifted at domestic things, as her cousins were. They had always had to put things right for her, covering up, unpicking, supervising.

The rooms above the shop were quiet – Toby and Alexia had gone out.

She made some cocoa with the last of the milk, and sipped it slowly, with a sense of luxury. Then she took the empty bottle downstairs, rinsed it, and put it outside the back door.

Toby and Alexia's sitting-room door was closed. Very softly, as if they were somewhere in the house and might hear, she opened it. She stepped into the room and glanced round, her loneliness in some way eased by the evidence of other people's lives about her. Although the room was familiar enough to her, there were things she had always wanted to have a closer look at – especially the photograph of their beautiful, dark-haired, drooping-mouthed mother in her nineteen-twenties dress, and with a long bead necklace looped through her fingers. She had an expression, Cressy thought, of knowing that she would have to die and leave her darlings. She studied the photograph for some time, not touching it, almost like a burglar avoiding leaving any fingerprints. Then she turned to other objects. Books she skimmed over, not much interested in reading. There was a framed sampler, with the name *Alice Moorhead* done in cross-stitch.

Even looking at her own face in someone else's glass made a change. She smoothed her hair. Yes, she was pale and peaky, as they had said. She blew out her cheeks and banged them. Then she wandered on round the room, now laying her hands on things, for company. On the pinewood dresser, which had just come in from a sale, was a row of bottles. She pulled out corks and sniffed. Whisky. She recoiled from that one, and from rum, pushing the corks back quickly. Vodka. She tried that one with especial interest. It sounded exotic to her; but was nothing: disappointing. Cointreau – really delicious, this one. She lingered over it, sniffing deeply, with pleasure.

Suddenly there was a rattling on the shop door-handle. She started in terror, tried to ram back the cork into the bottle, missed it, tipped the bottle, and the sticky liquid was spilled down her skirt, some on the pale-wood dresser, some on the carpet.

David continued to rattle the door-handle and he stooped down and called through the letter-box. When he straightened his back, he saw through the glass panel of the door, a pale shape gliding slowly towards him through the dark shop, coming between the pieces of furniture like a sleep-walker.

Cressy seemed to look right through him as she opened the door. 'They're out,' she said.

'What on earth's the matter?' he asked. There was quite a

smell of alcohol about her, and he wondered if she were drunk. Then he saw the wet patch on her dress.

'What's happened?' he asked.

'I shall have to run away,' she said.

He shut the door behind him and drew her farther inside, away from the glances of people coming home from church. 'You only need mopping up,' he said, 'as far as I can make out.'

'I shouldn't have touched it. I only wanted to find out what it was like, from the smell. I wouldn't have drunk any. You do believe that, don't you?'

'Of course.'

When he had got some of the story out of her, he asked. 'What were you doing in their room anyway, when they were out?'

'Well, when they are in, I can't have a proper look at any-thing. And I was lonely.'

This was beyond him.

'I can never explain it to them. They will think I creep down when their backs are turned and help myself to their drink.'

'Well, I don't think they will think that. I shall make sure they don't. Let's mop the mess up, and I'll explain it to them, if you like.'

'They won't be back till late.'

'Well, I'll still explain it somehow.'

'And I've wasted all that. However much worth, do you think?'

'Oh, a little goes a long way, you know. Don't worry. Run and fetch a wet cloth.'

He went into the sitting-room and looked round. When Cressy came back with the cloth, she said, 'That dresser! It's really for stock.' She had a great awe of stock – spoiling any of it being so much on her mind.

He took the cloth from her, for she seemed incapable of

75

doing anything sensible, and he swabbed the dresser and the carpet. 'When that's dry, it won't show a mark,' he said confidently. He felt disposed to add, 'Least said, soonest mended,' but decided she might think less of him for giving such advice. To make a clean breast of it she was plainly determined, now that she no longer seemed to be thinking of running away. And he could understand how alarming Toby and Alexia might seem to her – cold in their self-sufficiency; their indifference verging on callousness.

He knelt down and began to sponge the skirt of her dress. 'Not much damage there, either,' he said cheerfully. 'Hang it up somewhere to dry, and put on something else, and I'll take you out for a drink.' After all, I did promise them I would, he remembered. He had been so busy, though, that it had gone out of his mind. Even at week-ends, he had had no time, feeling new responsibilities towards his mother, and taking her out to dinner, or having little parties at home. Nell Stapleforth had come down once or twice. She had given up the idea of David as a husband, but liked her dog to get into the country.

Cressy had seemed to flinch at the word 'drink', so he added, 'Or anywhere else you'd care to go.'

'Could we go to a Wimpy Bar?' she asked, her expression suddenly eager.

Oh, my God! he thought. All those youths with studded leather jackets; ghastly smell of fried onions. 'On a Sunday, surely they're all closed,' he said. 'And we'd have to go into the town, and I don't want to be away too long. My mother's on her own.'

'Then couldn't we go and see your mother?' she asked, just as eagerly. 'I like her so much.'

'I didn't know you knew her. But that's fine.' To be able to kill two birds with one stone was David's idea of luck. 'Wimpy

Bar another day,' he said. 'The car's outside. Get moving. Run and change your dress.'

Cressy had no intention of appearing before Midge in Quayne clothes, shabby as her shop-bought dress was. 'I haven't another,' she explained. 'I think this will dry quite quickly, though.'

She stood before Midge's bright, crackling fire, and held out her steaming skirt. 'My dreams have come true,' she said, looking round the room. She had made up pictures in her mind of such a room, full of pretty things, and nothing hand-woven in it.

'I'm sure you'll think it very odd,' she told Midge, 'but I had never seen coal burning before I went to live at the shop. At school, we only had radiators, and at home we just have wood, and it usually seems to be damp and won't get going at all; then it suddenly flares up for a minute or two. Even in the pub, they have that electric thing with imitation coal. My father and Father Daughtry make speeches about it, but they make speeches about everything – the price of the Guinness and not having proper draught beer. And frozen food. They all go on about *that* at Quayne. Well, I don't agree. I bought a little packet of peas, and thought they were the nicest I ever had in my life. And no trouble, and no maggots.' Her skirt seemed to have dried, and she looked about in contentment. 'So you just live here together? How nice that must be. I hear your husband left you,' she said in a polite tone to Midge.

'Yes, he upped and went.'

'What would you like to drink?' David asked Cressy.

'I'd very much like a cocktail, please,' she said airily. David looked gravely at Midge, who was bringing him some glasses. They did not smile.

Midge was enjoying her evening. The girl's naiveté drew the

older ones close together in complicity. They shared her, and quite delighted in her. They really could hardly believe in her.

'And you have a television set,' she said wonderingly.

Midge thought it spoilt the room and it was half hidden in a corner behind an étagère with pots of fern and white cyclamen.

'I've seen it in shop windows,' Cressy said. 'My grandfather was on it once. But he always said "I appear on it, but I don't have it".'

She seemed so happy, sipping her drink, enjoying the heat of the coal fire; but, once, she sighed sharply, looking at David with frightened eyes, suddenly remembering.

'Don't let it spoil your evening,' he said. 'I shall do all the explaining for you. I promise it will be all right.'

'I shouldn't *bother* to explain,' said Midge, who had been told the story. 'There's no harm done. Why drag it up?'

'But the drink I wasted,' Cressy said. 'It's so terribly expensive.'

'That won't worry *them*. They're all right.'

Cressy turned questioningly to David. 'Rather my own sentiments, I must confess,' he said.

'Then if you two say so, I am sure it is right,' Cressy said in a relieved voice. 'I shall just enjoy this beautiful cocktail and forget it.'

As it was Sunday evening, Midge said that they would have supper by the fire. There was a creamy dish of braised kidneys, a cheese in a little wooden box, and a plate of figs arranged on vine-leaves. They drank claret, and she told them about the Monsignors. She told them a great deal about Quayne, chattering happily, with colour in her cheeks. Midge was deeply interested.

When it was time for David to take Cressy home, Midge went out to the door with them. 'Oh, it is almost winter,' she said, standing in the porch, shivering. 'You must be frozen, child.' She touched Cressy's bare arm. 'Come again, won't you, and cheer me up, for the long dark days I can't abide.'

'Oh, I will,' Cressy said. She felt vindicated now in the steps she had taken. Life was beginning to open up as she had promised herself it would. Sometimes, lately, during the day's routine of cleaning and customers, and the evening's loneliness, she had almost despaired. But she had held on, and now was rewarded.

'Your mother's marvellous,' she told David, as they drove away.

'I think so.'

'She seems so young. To be able to have clothes like that . . .' she sighed, but more in wonderment than envy.

'I hardly ever go in a car,' she said. 'It's so enjoyable.' Harry Bretton had a very old Rolls-Royce, and she and her cousins had always been driven to the station in it to catch the train for school. Otherwise, it was rarely taken out of its barn. It was consequently very damp and smelled of fungus.

'I always wanted to ask you,' Cressy began. 'I heard what you said about me that day in the shop, when you came in with that friend of yours with the dog. Why did you call me "bothersome"? I've never been to you. It was the other way round. That thing you wrote bothered me dreadfully.'

David felt that he was always making amends to her. 'You shouldn't listen to other people's conversations,' he said feebly.

'But *am* I bothersome?'

'I don't know,' he said, after a pause. 'But don't keep putting me in the wrong, or we'll never be friends.'

As they reached the valley, she became quiet again.

'If you're sure you think I needn't say anything . . .'

'Now, forget it,' he said sternly. 'Stop making mountains out of mole-hills. You must know by now that Toby and Alexia loathe a fuss.'

'All right,' she said contentedly. 'It's been such a wonderful evening – the nicest of my life, I think.'

David could not help being pleased at the idea of having given someone the nicest evening of her life. Most of the girls he knew would not have dreamed of saying so, if it were true.

Cressy was a little disappointed that he did not suggest a date for their next meeting; but, all the same, she went happily to bed.

David was back home in no time, before Midge had finished clearing up. Usually when he took girls home, she would go to bed and to sleep, and not see him again until morning.

'You go out into the highways and by-ways and bring me back some delightful entertainment,' Midge said.

'Yes, but we could soon have that one round our necks.'

'"I hear your husband left you." Didn't you adore that? No one's ever said it to me before. They do sound such a rum lot up there, at Quayne. It's practically medieval.'

'They're a rum lot all right. Well, I think I'll go up now. I must make an early start tomorrow. For I'm off to Little Gidding in the morning,' he began to sing, but then stopped, and looked anxiously at her. 'Only two days. You'll be all right, will you?'

'Of course,' she said brightly. It would be got over, she thought.

For the rest of her life, this responsibility, he was thinking. Of all things, responsibility he seemed to resent the most. It should be her husband's concern, he told himself crossly, going upstairs to bed.

CHAPTER EIGHT

'I have always wanted to get into a fast set,' Cressy said. She was breathless from her Charleston lesson with Midge. David was sorting out records for them. At his age, he thought he should give up dancing. Too self-conscious now to shake and shudder with the teenagers, he felt that he belonged to a bygone age of dances in which the sexes were clasped together, cheeks touching – and even conversation, however banal, was carried on. 'Do you come here often?' and all those jokes of long ago; but one had to say something. The memories were sobering and ageing.

Midge, however, had risen above these considerations: nor was she now the least bit breathless. Still under the spell of the rhythm, she flung her little heels out sideways, and her elbows, she crossed and re-crossed her hands on her pink-trousered knees, all angles, like a puppet.

'I haven't enjoyed myself so much with my clothes on,' she declared, recalling the old times, when she had often said that and raised a smile – those days when everyone had been scared of her, and Archie had come courting, with his talk of poetry and romance, and winning her, she now most furiously realised, with quotations from Rupert Brooke – and, of course, by being a cut above car salesmen and brewers' representatives; better educated; better off. To have been taken in by Rupert Brooke annoyed her most of all. 'If you look like that, you don't have to be a good poet,' she said nowadays, for she was very sensitive to what was currently admired.

David was a little put out by the change in his mother. Cressy seemed to have gone to her head, and he wished she had not used the last phrase in front of her.

'Now what?' she asked, and said to Cressy, 'You're doing very well.'

Archie had been no good as a dancer. He had trundled her about. She ought to have been warned by that; for dancing and sex were linked, she knew, not only in her mind, but in the minds of far cleverer people – she had leafed a bit through Freud, looking for other things – and Archie, she had soon discovered trundled through sex.

Cressy was wearing trousers, too – pale yellow ones, the colour of her hair. Midge had given them to her, saying she had outgrown them, and Cressy, in her endeavours to get them on, had cast buttons all over the place – so that Midge had the pleasure of her gratitude and the pleasure of the scattered buttons as well.

To David and Midge, having Cressy about was like having a marvellous child to care for. They were perpetually under the excitement of giving treats. Sometimes, he felt that they were almost like grandparents, with a world to bestow and not too much responsibility. Very *young* grandparents. Dancing grandmother.

He put on a tango and then wished that he had not. Once Midge had done a burlesque tango with Jack Ballard. They had all thought it amusing at the time – apache stuff, rose clenched in teeth, back bends, snarling, stamping. But they had been drunk at the time; now he was not.

His mother was transformed by being admired. She, who had always looked quite young, looked five or ten years younger.

'I can't . . . I can't . . . keep up,' gasped Cressy, flinging herself on to the sofa. The tango had not got very far.

'Oh, this is the nadir of life,' she said, reaching for her drink.

'The nadir?'

'Yes, don't you know, the nadir of the gods. I've heard my father talk of it.'

Midge smiled at David more warmly than he at her.

The drinks he gave Cressy were more grenadine than anything, and they always seemed to suffice; but he was not sure of his mother's mixtures, and this evening Cressy had been there before he arrived. She very often was.

He wondered if she ought to be discouraged from coming so often. If his mother tired of her, it would be a sudden thing, and there would be no going back on it, and only heartbreak or deep bewilderment for the girl. At present she seemed so happy – equally happy with his mother or himself. Sometimes, he had taken her out alone, calling for her when the shop closed on Saturdays, and he had found himself, to his amusement, in all kinds of strange places he would never have dreamed of going to without her – sitting in coffee-bars, for instance, among bamboo, plastic vines and fishing-nets, while the juke-box never let up and the coffee-machine gasped and gurgled, and all round him was the younger generation. Her pleasure in such places was unbelievable. She looked about her with shining eyes. And there were all the other places, where they ate hamburgers and there was much the same din and an overpowering smell of onions frying; or where there were fruit machines, or ten-pin bowling. They had high-teas in depressing cinema cafés. He had even had to take her into a launderette on their way home late one night, to have a look round. He often felt foolish, but was too amused to mind. He also felt much older. But her enchantment was something not to be missed – her falling in love with the present time.

This evening of the dancing, he was very quiet. He knew that Cressy had changed – he had watched her changing – and it had been his theory that people never did. All his father said about his mother in the old days he discounted as the errors of an old man's rancorous memory. In his own eyes, Midge had always been the same. Yet Cressy had altered, and in a very moving way. It was not just a matter of the yellow trousers or the made-up eyes (for she was no longer waifish); but she was all in blossom, as if the spring had come. She was like an indulged pet, who responded with the warmest affection. She suggested a confidence in the world that was almost alarming to him.

They had dinner. Midge now seemed to find it more of a satisfaction to cook for Cressy's praise than David's. Anything the girl liked especially was bound to reappear.

'Meat on Friday,' Cressy said with satisfaction, when she had finished her steak. 'I have never had it before.'

'Oh, my dear . . .' Midge said, as if she were appalled . . . 'I simply didn't think.'

'But why not have it? I never saw the sense of that. What's the difference between fish and meat, anyhow. One's no more of a treat than the other, and they're both the flesh of dead creatures.'

'Oh, Cressy, please,' said David, who ate more slowly.

'You should have reminded me,' Midge said. 'Now I feel like the devil himself.'

'Are you religious?' Cressy asked, in a rather suspicious voice.

'That's a bit difficult to answer. Of course, one knows it must all have had a beginning . . .'

'Do you go to Church?'

'Well, I've always thought . . . whatever one's vague ideas . . .

one can do just as much good without going. I know I try to, if I say it myself.'

'Then you're not,' Cressy said, and sounded relieved.

Later, when David had taken Cressy home, Midge lay in bed, listening for his car. She had begun to feel nervy and agitated, and could not explain to herself why.

He shouldn't keep her out so late, she thought. After all, *she* has to work in the morning, if he hasn't, she rationalised. All words of calm reason, she decided. But she was not calm. She was angry with David. She's so young, she kept telling herself. And at the back of her mind, a voice said nastily, 'Now they will have secrets *you* cannot share.'

In the morning, he said nothing, but to suggest Nell Stapleforth's paying a visit the following week-end.

So what has gone wrong? Midge wondered, keeping fairly silent herself. If something had happened, and she was never to see Cressy again, she would find it difficult to forgive him. He would have taken away the only fun she had nowadays, and condemned her to be alone again for all those slow-going hours.

She spent a wretched day, waiting for a mention of Cressy that never came, looking for signs in him, clues in his behaviour, but he simply carried on in a null way, working most of the time in his room, finishing an article.

It was an almost soundless day, damp, still. Midge was on her own downstairs, and thought the hours would never go by.

Self-pity, the despised emotion, so difficult to overcome, set in as did the promised fog rising from the valley. Four o'clock in the afternoon she had always hated. There was no sound from upstairs. A bird squawked briefly in the garden, the thinnest of noises, with all of winter in it.

Where will he go this evening, she wondered.

He went nowhere. He looked at the television but as if

seeing nothing, and was just as boring as his father had ever been.

On Wednesday afternoon, which was Cressy's half-day, she arrived at half past three, carrying a parcel. She looked forlorn once more.

'It's for you,' she told Midge, when she had held one blue hand to the fire for a moment.

'For me? You ought to wear gloves, my dear. You'll get chilblains.'

'I wanted to give it to you ages ago, but I've only just managed to save up for it.'

It was true. What she had deprived herself of in the last weeks, Midge would never guess.

'You mustn't give me presents,' Midge said, looking mystified, as she untied the string. She unwrapped the Wedgwood wedding group.

'My dear,' she said gravely, 'this you should never have done.'

'Why not? You gave me everything. I didn't want to think it had been that way round all the time.'

'Gave,' Midge noted; and 'had been'. So no more was to be given?

'My dear child, it must have cost the earth. I feel terrible about it.'

'Well, don't,' Cressy said. 'It was quite expensive but I got it cheaper than a customer would. I think it's pretty hideous, but you admired it the first time I met you.'

'So I did. I remember. Oh, it's the most lovely present I ever had. Let me put it against this red wall. There, it looks so beautiful. Is that where you would like to see it when you come in?'

'I shan't be coming in. David wants it all to stop.'

'Wants what to stop?'

'My coming here, and being bothersome. That's a word he has for me.'

She began to cry and Midge, who did not know about her weakness for tears, could not have believed the girl could look so pitiful, with her shoulders hunched, her thin hands covering her face, her hair falling forwards.

'It was my fault,' Cressy said, fumbling up her sleeve for her handkerchief, and then smothering her face with it.

Midge let her cry for a while and then asked, hardly breathing, 'What happened? I think you should tell me.'

'It was on Friday. Going home that night, through the woods, I asked him why he didn't make love to me. I thought men always did when they had girls in cars, and it was dark. I was worried that he never seemed to think of it. I wanted so much to try it. I never have,' she said, looking at Midge, showing her red and swollen face for a moment. 'Am I so awful? I felt I had every right to find out.'

'You know,' Midge began, and paused. She was rather taken aback, and could not at once think of anything to say. 'Perhaps there's nothing so dangerous as having led a sheltered life.'

'But it was only from experience I was sheltered. I know a great deal about sex, as I explained to David. Some of my grandfather's books have to be seen to be believed. When he and my grandmother went up to Buckingham Palace to get his C.B.E., I read them all day long, and tried to work out the illustrations. Of course, my mother told me when I was little, but I never thought she had much idea. But those books were an eye-opener. I thought to myself, if it's as complicated as that, I'd better get the hang of it, so that I don't feel a complete idiot when the occasion arises.'

At the thought of the pornographic books, she had stopped crying. She rubbed her wet cheeks like a child.

'I think you would have been better off with just your

87

mother's explanation,' Midge said. 'She wouldn't have left out love. Of course, I don't know what books they were, but I can guess.'

She could, for her own father had had them hidden away, and she herself had snooped when young. She was quite shocked that a religious man like Harry Bretton, a national figure, should sink to the level of Bertie Reynolds and the Outriders, or some of those regulars in the saloon bar when she was young, slipping folded papers from their wallets and slyly handing them round. It was quite disgraceful.

'They are artistic books,' Cressy said with dignity.

'Yes, I dare say. But you try to forget them, my dear. When you get married, that will be the time to make your discoveries. It will be as simple as can be, and mugging up all those acrobatics you'll see was quite unnecessary.'

She sounded just like Rose, Cressy thought in horror.

'And, meanwhile,' Midge went on, 'you'd better not go about offering yourself to young men. They might not all have David's sense of responsibility.' Then could have wished the words unsaid, for she knew nothing of what had really happened that night, and he had been a very long time coming home. She felt rather foolish, lit a cigarette and waited.

'I can read your thoughts,' Cressy said. That Rose-like speech had made her hostile. 'I assure you that your dear son was just as upright as you hope he was. It was I who made a fool of myself.'

'Not irreparably,' Midge said.

'I've ruined our friendship, that's all I know, and it was the only thing I had. He never wants to see me again.'

'Oh, nonsense!'

'Well, I never want to see him again.'

'He probably feels that he put you in a false position. After all, he's years older than you.'

'And so was your husband years older than you.'

88

'But look at that poor little marriage . . .'

'Why bring marriage into it?'

'Darling, stop skating about and being cross. I'll speak to David. May I? I know him so well, and I know that responsibility scares him stiff. But there's no earthly reason why you shouldn't be friends again.'

'I'm too ashamed to want to meet him again ever.'

'Don't play theatres, darling. I'm going to make some tea now. At least I know that's the right thing to do.'

Cressy was crying again, and angrily dashing away tears.

On her way out of the room, Midge paused to look again at the wedding group. 'I love it so much,' she said.

'I find I miss the child,' David said, sitting down by the fire after dinner, looking worn-out, as if eating the meal had exhausted him. 'And the very *thought* of Nell coming down on Friday. I wish I'd never asked her.' His life seemed suddenly too tedious for words.

Embarrassment can be both tiring and confusing. The conversation about Cressy had made him feel like a shying horse. It was not a fit subject for mother and son to discuss.

'If I hadn't cared about her, I'd have laughed it off and never have stopped the car,' he confessed.

'*Cared* about her?' Midge asked in astonishment. She had not bargained for this. She quickly righted her voice, and went on as if the question had not been asked, and it was not answered. 'She *was* put out,' she said lightly.

'Yes, so you said. It's all unbelievable. Girls like that shouldn't be let loose. She makes me feel so bloody old, too. I find myself talking to her like a Dutch uncle, whatever they may be.'

'I know. I find myself doing much the same.'

But Midge had enjoyed the experience. It had been rather a pleasant change, and she had felt so completely in authority.

'Drinking again,' David said, watching her dully. 'I can't think what my father would say.'

Midge smiled; but she knew that his remark, which he might have made on any other evening, this time sprang from hostility.

Serious matters they had always approached lightly. There had not been so very many of them, but the worries that had occurred had been treated in an offhand, amused manner. It will all come out in the wash. Indeed they had no other manner with one another. For this reason, she had talked of Cressy's visit and her confession, as if it were rather absurd; entertaining, certainly. Intuitive though she usually was with him, it had been a little time this evening before she realised that he was not smiling, might even be angry at her flippancy. He thought the subject should not have been broached – there had been too much talking altogether – and he wished that Cressy had kept her mouth shut, had stayed away, in fact. Midge could not coax him into laughter.

So now she was pouring herself out a drink and trying to think of something quite different to talk about. All would fall into place, she was sure. She would be able to manœuvre them out of this dangerous situation. Nell's coming that week-end would be a help, whatever David might think at this moment, and Midge began to wonder how she could make a very special time of it, to put right this evening's misunderstanding – and that, of course, to her, meant in the way of creature comforts. She fetched a cookery book – always, these days, her favourite reading – and as she turned the pages, she could sense his stillness, as he sat sprawled in his chair, staring at the fire. Then the stillness was suddenly broken. 'I think I'll go down for a pint,' he said, getting up abruptly.

'I came to ask Cressy out for a drink.'

Toby held the door open wide. 'A splendid idea,' he said.

'Alexia just said that we should invite her down and we were both wondering how we decently could not. However, we had this very minute decided that we mustn't leave her up there crying on her own another evening – no matter what conditions we had at the beginning. You see,' he said, opening the door of the sitting-room, 'we are not entirely heartless – though very nearly. He has come in the nick of time, Alexia.'

She looked up with relief from peeling a pear. The remains of supper were on the table, wine-glasses, a plateful of walnut shells, and opened books – a scene of easy peacefulness. David could understand what a sacrifice they had been about to make.

'Yes, we are very nearly heartless,' Alexia agreed.

'What is all this crying?' David asked.

'It's worse than ever, I can tell you.'

'Oh, come off it, David,' Toby protested. 'She is a love-sick wraith. You've started something you know, and we are suffering for it. We think you are very nearly heartless, too.'

'And for the slipperiest customer we've ever known,' Alexia said calmly, 'we find this entanglement surprising.'

'Entanglement? What has the child got into her head now?'

There was no need for a reply, and Alexia began to eat her pear.

'I'll go and ask her,' David said. 'But perhaps she won't want to come.'

This seemed to need no answer, either. Toby looked longingly at his open book. 'I'm afraid she may be rather a tear-stained little thing for the Horseshoes. But no doubt she can blot herself and put on a dash of powder.'

'If she wants, I will lend her my dark spectacles,' Alexia offered.

Cressy opened her door, holding some knitting in her hand. She was very much taken aback at seeing David, and said incoherently, 'It won't come right. I have to keep unpicking it.' She put the knitting to her eyes, and turned away. The room looked like some old-age pensioner's last, lonely refuge.

'Well, forget it for now,' he said, 'and let's go for a drink.'

'How can I, looking like this?' she asked dramatically.

'Alexia said she'd lend you her dark glasses.'

'So you've been talking about me. How, for God's sake, did *they* know my knitting had gone wrong?'

'It's not your knitting that's gone wrong – or if it has,' – he looked doubtfully at the strange-shaped thing she was holding – 'if it is, that's not what's troubling you.'

'I don't want to go to the Horseshoes. Father Daughtry might be there.'

'Well, we can go somewhere else, somewhere a bit farther on to give you more time to recover. You don't look too bad, anyway. Nothing that a bit of powder won't put right.'

'I look terrible.'

She really did. He picked up a brush and began to smooth her tangled hair, while she stood before the little looking-glass, her knees bent so that she could see into it, and dabbed her face with a grubby powder-puff. Very gently, he took her long hair in one hand, and brushed it with the other, loosening the snarls without at all hurting her. He imagined her lying on the bed weeping, tangling her hair against the pillow, and he was very moved and contrite.

'Why did you come?' she asked, and her eyes suddenly glittered again and looked about to spill over.

'Come along, or it will be closing-time.'

'You only think about drink,' she said, smiling for the first time.

'Well, I'm not going to one of your Wimpy Bars at this hour of the day. I've had my dinner.'

Then, as he turned away to put the brush down, he saw on the chest of drawers a plate with some crumbs, and the silver foil from a triangle of processed cheese, and he suddenly thought about her present to Midge. 'Unless you're hungry,' he said.

'I couldn't eat a thing.'

'You know, you shouldn't have given that present to my mother. It was far too expensive.'

She pushed the plate out of sight angrily. 'I can read you like a book,' she said.

Although, as they passed the Three Horseshoes, Father Daughtry was getting ponderously into a car to be driven up Quayne Hill by one of his cronies, they did not go in. It certainly would be too embarrassing, David thought – with Cressy's eyes still red with crying.

Once, she had imagined that the very limit of bliss would be to drive in such a car as this, with someone like David; now it was not enough. She sat, with her hands folded in her lap, staring ahead of her at the light fog drifting across the blurred light from the headlamps.

He was making for another pub called The Squirrel, but before they reached it she had begun to cry again, so he drove on. He was surprised to find himself touched and distressed, and not irritated, by her tears.

'You do seem nervy,' he said.

'I am trying to give up biting my nails and it is quite a strain,' she said, clasping her hands tightly.

'Oh, I should bite them,' he advised kindly.

'And I was trying so hard, for your sake,' she said.

'Don't let's go to any pub,' he said. 'Drink isn't really all I think about. It just makes a sort of pattern in one's life, as other things don't seem to.'

He wanted a pattern so much, and for the first time consciously knew it.

He stopped the car under some trees, and she looked up apprehensively.

'Cressy, darling, will you marry me?' he asked, almost to his own astonishment.

She drew in her breath as if aghast, and leaned away from him. He felt her staring in his direction.

Waiting for her answer, he realised that he knew nothing about her; and he was frightened, either way, of how she would reply. She began to bite her nails.

There was a long silence, in which he almost wished to start up the car and pretend that nothing extraordinary had happened. Then she said, in a pinched voice, 'But are you sure I shan't be an inconvenience to you?'

CHAPTER NINE

David and Nell went on their Sunday afternoon walk in the damp countryside, down lanes between holly bushes choked with dead beech-leaves, under the singing, hissing electric pylons, in another direction from Quayne. Each time a car came by, she snatched up her dog, and held it to her bosom, and glared, backing into the hedge. 'What on earth are they doing, driving about on a Sunday afternoon?' she complained.

'Taking Mother for a spin,' he suggested.

Because of all the cars, they seemed to be walking in single-file most of the time. He suggested taking a short cut home through the woods, where she stumbled over brambles, cursing, clutching her dog, and laddering her stockings.

Holding back a thorny branch for her, he said, 'I want to tell you, Nell, that Cressy and I are going to be married.'

She stopped, and stared at him.

'Cressy? That little girl?'

'Cressy. That little girl.'

He pulled the branch back farther, impatient for her to get on, and discomfited by her stare.

'You must be joking,' she said, not moving a step forward.

'I am in dead earnest.'

'My God, your mother will go up the wall.'

He looked at her with what he meant to be an expression of disdain. 'I don't know what you mean.'

'You bloody do, old dear.'

'I had to get married some time,' he said, betraying his understanding.

'And often I've wondered how you were going to manage it.'

'As a matter of fact, I haven't told her yet.'

'I can understand that.'

At last, she moved on, and he could let go of the bough.

'I haven't told anyone, in fact,' he said.

When they came to the edge of the wood, she heaved herself up on the stile, large and ungainly, all bent legs, like a cow getting up, he thought. 'You could knock me down with a feather,' she declared.

As they neared home, she said, 'Well, I'm looking forward to my tea.' She pictured the fire, the buttered toast, and all her delightful new speculations about poor, unwary Midge.

Rose took up her usual place by the window, so that she could look out of it, when she could not trust herself to face the others.

David addressed himself to Joe, who roamed about, rolling one cigarette after another, continually relighting them, or twisting them, unlit, in his fingers. Cressy, who had refused to be left out of this drama, sat on a stool by the fire, looking interested and excited.

She was of an age when David felt he must ask permission to marry her. Never, for any of his other girl-friends would he have done that, and he was feeling like someone from a bygone age.

He could tell that his request had come as a relief to Joe, but Rose's reaction was another matter.

'But . . . I'm very sorry, it sounds so rude,' she began, turning briefly from the rain-covered window. 'It is all such a shock, such a surprise. We don't even know you.' Her own husband had practically been chosen for her, so that she had been sure all was in order.

'I hope you will come to see my mother very soon,' David said stiffly.

'Yes, of course. I believe we are quite neighbours. But, at Quayne, we seem so self-sufficient, we rarely visit.'

'Cressy and I want to live near here,' David said soothingly. 'We cannot go very far away, for my mother's sake. She will be quite alone when I go.'

'Your father is dead?'

'My father and mother are separated.'

He might as well have thrown in bankruptcy, syphilis, congenital madness, haemophilia, indecent exposure, treason and fraud. From the expression on her face, it seemed no more could make a difference to Rose.

'I'm glad you think of your mother,' she said, with her back turned to Cressy.

Harry would have to be told, she thought. And who was going to do that?

'And where will you be married?' she asked fearfully.

David understood that these words were the only permission he would be given.

'Neither Cressy nor I have any religion. We shall go to the registry office in Market Harbury,' he said.

And then Rose moved to a chair and sat down, thinking her legs would support her no longer.

Midge – but she did not know – was the third one to be told of the engagement, and on this occasion, Cressy was not allowed to be part of the drama; although, as it turned out, if she had been there, she would have thought the way it was played very right and proper, and what could have been expected, and so unlike the bleak performance in her own home.

Before dinner one evening, David, feeling doomed and self-conscious, stripped off the wrapping from a bottle of champagne, and then broached both the bottle and the news.

His mother's pleasure was more than he could have imagined. She seemed quite shocked with joy. Her lips trembled so that she was scarcely able to say how delighted she was, and tears – unbelievably – brimmed her eyes.

'You must forgive me,' she said, wiping them away, 'for it is such a very special evening.'

She, like Rose, turned aside for a moment, and she put her glass down before she had taken a sip.

'So fizzy!' she explained, when she picked it up again. She wrinkled her nose, and then said, 'To you both, darling!' and drank a little. 'Oh, heavens, what a happy thing,' she added.

Taking her glass with her she went into the kitchen to look into the oven. She stayed there for as long as she could. Her hands were very cold, and her mind confused. For once, she let something burn.

'In my excitement,' she explained.

After dinner, she said, 'Will you take me out for another celebration drink?' She had never before asked him to take her out; but she knew that she could not be at home alone that evening, not even at home alone with him. Only when she was safely in bed, with the light out, could she face anything, or be herself again.

'Yes, let's do that,' David said eagerly. 'Shall I fetch your coat? We'll go down and get Cressy and Toby and Alexia, and celebrate.'

*

On a Wednesday evening, neither French nor Italian day, David went to see his father. This time, Archie was not cleaning silver, but arranging some whiting, tails in mouth, for frying.

A very old wireless-set was on in the kitchen. Through sounds like gales roaring and twigs crackling, Archie had been listening to the weather-forecast. It was just coming to an end. 'There may even be some dry spells in the South,' a callous voice announced. Archie switched it off.

'They always break their promises,' he said. 'That's one thing I couldn't do.'

'You broke the biggest one of all,' David said. 'You promised to love, cherish and whatever it is your future wife.'

'That was in church, and the words were put into my mouth, almost one by one, as if I couldn't take in a whole sentence at a time. It was very galling. I was in an appallingly false position. Such a coarse service – "for the procreation of children" and so on. Well, they were procreated all right. For my sins.' He chuckled. 'I should have preferred to have been married in a registry office. But your mother wanted this comic opera display.'

'Yes, I've heard about that before. Well, I shall do better than you, for I am *really* going to be married in a registry office.'

'I am glad to have had a little influence,' Archie said in a casual voice. He studied the whiting with pride and interest. 'We usually have fish on Wednesdays. It's a good day for it. How is she?' he asked, when he had floured the two fish and put them aside. 'Your mother?'

'She is a responsibility I feel very keenly.'

'I can imagine *that*. You really ought to get married, you know.'

'I *am* going to get married.'

'Although it's a vicious circle. Marriage ruined me, and to stop *yourself* being ruined, you feel you must go and run the

99

same risk. Is there no alternative? Now you have made *me* feel responsible.'

'I'm very glad to hear it.'

'I only hope your wife will get up for breakfast. Properly up, I mean. Shipshape and Bristol fashion. I can remember to this day that horrible quilted dressing-gown that would never fasten in the front. She was the first and only slut I ever knew. *Breakfast*, I said. A strange word to describe that horrid brew and a piece of squeaky cold toast.'

Oh, his cankered, aggrieved old mind, David thought. The enormities of his imagination.

'Now that chore is chored,' Archie said with satisfaction, rinsing his hands at the sink, drying them, and drawing down the cuffs of his velvet jacket, 'so let us repair to rather less sordid surroundings. A glass of sherry in the drawing-room.'

In the drawing-room, an oil-stove gave out fumes, but no heat. While David fetched the sherry from the dining-room, Archie tucked a travelling-rug about his legs.

'You don't seem very much interested in my news,' David said.

'What news, my boy?'

'That I'm going to be married.'

'There's another rug on the sofa,' Archie said hospitably. 'I hope you're not after some money, you know. Much as I should like . . . but keeping your mother in gin has not exactly eased my situation. What with her gin, and this socialist government. Things daily go from bad to worse. I can't remember a time when I can look back and say, *then* we were decently governed.'

'Under Palmerston?'

Archie smiled his touching smile. 'I think you're teasing me; but I'm glad you know something of history. I believe so many of our troubles stem, much later, from the suffragettes.'

'Harry Bretton thinks so, too.'

'I can't place a Harry Bretton. My memory doesn't improve.'

'My future grandfather-in-law.'

'This is good news, dear boy. To marry into a family with sound ideas is what I did not do. They were in the hotel business . . .'

'I do know that much.'

'Of course, in the hotel business they are all Tories, but for the wrong reasons. For the feathering of the nest, and not for principles.'

'Father, don't you want to know about the girl I am going to marry?'

'Girl?' said Archie, looking alarmed, spilling some sherry on the travelling-rug. 'I hope you're not going to make my mistake, dear boy.'

'Your greatest mistake was in leaving Mother.'

'Never say it. Never say it.'

If he could mend his parents' marriage he could get on with his own in peace and with optimism, David had decided. Then he and Cressy could live in London, with her Wimpy Bars all round her, and his friends all about him, and his work near by.

Before he had left that morning, he had told Midge that he would be late home. 'I am going to see Father and tell him the news,' he had said. She had not answered. Greatly daring, he had asked, 'Any message?' (He can come home now, was all the message Midge could think of.) 'Kind regards, etcetera, etcetera,' she had said.

'You don't seem in the least interested in whom I'm going to marry,' David said to his father, in an offended tone of voice. 'Haven't even asked her name.'

'Well, what's her name, then? Out with it, young man.'

'Cressida Mary MacPhail.'

'"Cressida" is pretty. Yes, "Cressida" is very pretty. The surname sounds a bit wild; but, of course, you'll be altering that.'

'She's nineteen years old.'

'Her parents can't be in their right minds to consider it. I trust it will be a long engagement. Well, I give you my blessing for what it's worth, and I hope it won't turn out too badly for you. I think, in the circumstances, another glass of sherry, don't you?'

'But first I must nip up and see Aunt Sylvie. She should be speaking her own language today.'

'Don't linger and tire her, there's a good chap. And don't upset her with all this talk of marrying. She's really getting very frail – less and less and less of her, poor darling. I'll give you five minutes, and then I must fry my whiting.'

Upstairs, in her room, Aunt Sylvie was relabelling some of her possessions. David knocked on the door and was bidden to enter by a quavering, suspicious voice. She was just setting down a tortoiseshell box, whose label she had been altering – simply by crossing out one name and writing another. Underneath every piece of furniture or ornament, stuck behind pictures and inside box-lids were little gummed tickets, so that Archie would know where everything was to go when she died. He would not know, because some of the names were those of people who had died; but Aunt Sylvie had forgotten their deaths. She had, in fact, just been crossing off a great-nephew who had not been to see her for many years. Looking at an old photograph of him, Aunt Sylvie had suddenly got into a huff at being so neglected, forgetting all the grief there had been when the young man had been killed in the landings in Normandy.

David, not knowing what she had been doing, and for something to say, admired the tortoiseshell box. She stared him out grimly. No matter how he hinted or wheedled, his name would never be written on anything of hers, she thought. No use! No use! She whispered to herself, ducking her chin down, blowing into her bodice, for the room was very warm. Even that hussy, his mother, she remembered, had not dared to try to curry favour and cadge things out of her. Unless she now had changed her ways, and sent him foraging.

David was glad that he had been told to make a brief visit. She was very difficult to talk to. She had a regal manner of raising her eyebrows and shifting her eyes about, as if she had had enough of the conversation, and was waiting for a courtier to rid her of this troublesome kinsman.

He spoke of the weather, which had no meaning to her in that stuffy room, and he inquired after the Vicar, who Aunt Sylvie thought was none of his business. At the end of five minutes, he looked at his watch and said that he must go. 'And Father must fry the whiting, he said,' he added.

As he went to the door, Aunt Sylvie said nastily, 'Another time I should like you to remember that I prefer my dinner to be a surprise.'

PART TWO

CHAPTER TEN

So grim the garden was, with all the old cabbage stumps and the reeling line of beansticks.

'Grass it over,' Midge had said, determinedly optimistic, while Cressy and David stood dismayed. Neither of them loved the country, and this cottage seemed in the very depths of it and had, perhaps, for that reason, been empty since summer. Back from the road, across two fields and up a bumpy track it stood, and the nearest house was Midge's own. Throughout all their house-hunting, she had continued to see its possibilities, and every new bundle of circulars from estate-agents had seemed a threat to her.

Inside the cottage and in every room, she saw possibilities. Walls could be knocked down at little cost, or proofed against damp, and dreadful *art-nouveau* tiles round the sitting-room fireplace were so hideous that they were 'fun', she said. She suggested they might even be made a feature; and then added that it *was* only a suggestion, thinking she had made too many.

They had clumped dolefully upstairs and about the bare bedrooms. Even in the largest one there was no place to fit in a double bed. 'I shall get my chilblains again, going from one bed to the other,' Cressy said.

'I will get the chilblains,' David gallantly promised.

Midge looked aloof.

In the end, she had won all her points, and David and Cressy were married, and living in the cottage, and looking out, every day, at the tangled garden where, now, glossy young leaves of plants unknown to them were beginning to push up under a wilderness of brambles and dead growth.

Hand-woven curtains, a wedding-gift from Rose, hung at every window, and a white-painted surround strove to make a feature of the fireplace tiles, but no one was ever seen to be taken with mirth at the sight of them. The furniture was a strange jumble – resulting from David's mistakes, Cressy's apathy, and Midge's advice, discernment, and generosity. The effect was of everything cancelled out, and Toby and Alexia thought they had never seen such a conglomeration. Neither cosiness nor beauty had been achieved.

They – David and Cressy – had missed the worst of the winter there, they thought, but the cold and damp were bad enough during that early part of the year, and Cressy's chilblains came back. In the evenings, she sat by the fire and scratched her stockinged feet, while David tried to take her mind off them by stroking her hair and feeding her peppermint creams, as if she were his pet dog. He dreamed of a flat in London, and a fire to be switched on and off.

On Midge's visits – and she seldom at first came unless she were invited – her glances were all about her for ways of making improvements; and she brought chilblain ointments, and draught excluders, and ordered sweaters from the Isle of Aran, and never came empty-handed.

She was sometimes asked to dinner, and was quite wonderful about it, David thought. She would recall – as she sat before dinner with one drink after another – how long it had taken *her* to learn how to get potatoes done at the same time as the meat; and how on earth *could* one tell, she asked, if the apples under the piecrust were done or not. She chewed them valiantly, and even asked for more, murmuring 'delicious' – she, who had always pretended to eat to keep him company.

'I was quite frightened when she first came to dinner,' Cressy confessed one day to David, remembering how brussels sprouts had bobbed about in the boiling water and would not cook, and she had stood by the stove, trying to prong them with a fork, and crying. 'But she seems so appreciative.' She had gone back to her gas-ring food, which, in any case, she enjoyed more, and they had baked beans, and hamburgers from the shop, and tinned peas, and everything from then on seemed to her to go better.

Most things, apart from the awful garden, seemed to her to be going well; and that wilderness did not bother her, except that David lost his patience with it, and came indoors on Sundays from the hopeless battle, irritated and depressed.

Making love especially went well, she thought. In bed, she was what David described to himself as 'enthusiastic'. 'No holds barred,' she had said, the first time, in excited anticipation. Often, he wondered where she got all her ideas from, she was so full of bizarre suggestions. And, sometimes, he felt very old, as if he were no longer in the prime of life.

When he was away from home, she was never lonely, as he had feared. She drifted contentedly through the day, with a wonderful sense of freedom – and she had her television. This, unlike Midge's, was the focal point of the room. She looked at everything, beginning in the mornings, with perhaps Engineering Science for schools; then, as the day delightfully went on, there were programmes in Welsh, Flower-pot men for toddlers, racing, or Rugby Football, State Visits, puppets, quizzes, disasters, politicians, and old, old films of days before her time. She could hardly bear to get up to heat the beans, when David at last came home.

He hoped she would soon tire of it. Once, he wrote his name in the dust on top of the television-set, and she fetched a duster, and still stooping to watch a Highland reel, wiped it off.

When he was away for a night, she moved in with Midge and basked by the fire, and ate the lovely food, and so his absences were something neither of them minded.

The cottage fire was nothing like so cheerful as Midge's, and when the wind was the way it usually was, it smoked, and grime crept up the newly-painted walls, and chains of specks floated before their eyes as if their livers were disordered.

David decided that rural living was only tolerable if gracious and backed by plenty of money. His life was gracious no longer, and Cressy cooked breakfast in her old school dressing-gown, tied round her middle by a frayed cord.

Her inertia did not trouble her mother-in-law, who was quite unruffled at seeing the dressing-gown at eleven o'clock one morning. She had called to take Cressy shopping in the car, and she sat down calmly to wait. Then Cressy, re-tying the cord of her gown, said, 'Well, I only wanted a few potatoes and a packet of fish-cakes, so perhaps you could get them for me as I'm not ready.'

Midge, who had hoped for company, got up at once, with a nice smile, and left.

She knew all of Cressy's weaknesses, and foresaw the ones to come; for the new life was full of snares and opportunities – the dressing-gown, the dust, and, no doubt, in due time, a falling-off in looks. Midge used all her imagination on Cressy, not on her son, and when the girl came to stay, she would feed her with creamy sauces and brandied puddings, and there was always a little drink to hand.

'You mustn't stuff her up with all those things,' David protested one day, when he and Midge were alone. 'She's getting fat.'

'But she likes them, dear,' Midge said placidly, almost as if she hadn't heard.

And this morning, after buying the fish-cakes and the potatoes, she went to the Walnut Tree for a box of éclairs.

'I was wondering . . . how is your mother?' she asked when, later, she had returned to Cressy. She smoked, while Cressy ate an éclair.

'I don't know. She never comes to see me.'

'But *you* should go to see *her*,' Midge said, trying to laugh over the reproof. She rather missed the old stories about Quayne and, alone so much as she now was, would have liked the continuing saga to engage her thoughts. She had been once to Quayne, for what those there had called the wedding-breakfast – game pies and cold pheasant laid out on the table in the barn. It had been very different from the champagne-and-canapés weddings of her other sons, and she was the only one wearing a hat.

'That awful hill!' Cressy said, taking another éclair.

The next day, though, she made the great effort to please Midge, puffing up the hill, her breath blown back horribly, like moist fur, against her face. Everything dripped. There was this sound, and someone a way off felling a tree, and her own heavy breathing, and the commotion from starlings gathered over a ploughed field on the horizon. They looked like tea-leaves in the watery-grey distance, Cressy thought, and she could almost imagine the sky slowly turning brown from them. Here and there, leaves of a glossy, venomous green, splodged with black stains, poked up through the dead leaves under the hedges.

'I'll have to walk all this way back,' she told herself forlornly.

But she was doing her duty and this – as it does to people who do their duty very seldom – brought a surprising exhilaration.

'You mustn't let your mother think *I* have appropriated you,' Midge had said.

Cressy, plodding up the hill, could now hear voices on her right. Instead of a muffled, echoing sound from the middle of trees, these voices had clarity, floating away freely, as if from an open space; and, as she turned one of the bends in the lane, she saw a great clearing and the felled beeches lying about. There were shouts, a dry creaking noise which set Cressy's teeth on edge, and another tree crashed down across the low under-growth. She watched for a while, thinking the empty space a great improvement, letting the light in so, and wondered if it would be filled one day by willow-herb or bluebells.

Another figure was watching, from higher up on the ridge of the hill – her grandfather, in his shepherd's cloak. She moved nearer to the hedge and out of his sight, and waited there until he turned and moved away, back towards the house.

When she reached there, neither her mother nor her father was at home. Rather than go to look for them and risk all sorts of meetings, she took off her coat and made up the fire, and thought she would give them ten minutes, and then leave a note, and go, having – no one could deny – done her duty. She could not face her cousins at their weaving, nor the chance of running into her grandfather crossing the courtyard to the studio.

The simple room was very neat and clean and quiet. She stood by the fire, warming her hands, shifting her chilblained feet uneasily in her shoes, wondering why, after all, she had come. Simply to please Midge, she decided.

On the chimney-piece was a photograph of her wedding group, taken by Jack Ballard, after that peasant-like feasting in the barn she guessed that Midge had deplored. They were all arranged in the courtyard, with the chapel, as a reproach, in the background – the whole lot of them, with Cressy and David in the middle, and Harry Bretton, for once in his life, standing to one side. Midge was dressed in a dark suit and a white fur cap; the other women wore tweed coats and sensible shoes – they stood there sturdily, their hands in their pockets, their hair braided and coiled about their heads; they were making the best of a disappointing day. Father Daughtry looked owlish – perhaps the mulled wine, Cressy thought. It was rather touching of her mother to have framed the photograph and set it up in such an eye-catching place.

Cressy had dreaded Quayne having anything to do with her wedding day; but the right thing to be done had been pointed out to her, and she was overruled, even by Midge and David. It had to be, they explained to her, and, to her great surprise, had said that it was her mother's day as well.

During the brief proceedings at the registry office, Rose had felt sick, and trembled. It was not a true marriage to her, and she had no other child. Only she and Joe had come from Quayne. It was like, for special reasons, a very quiet funeral. And the others, at home, had prepared the feast in the same spirit, lugubriously and dutifully, as for mourners returning.

It was not at all like the Wedgwood wedding group, Cressy thought, looking at the photograph while she warmed her hands – no white dress, or flowers, or attendants.

Her father seemed glad to see her when he came in. Without stopping to wash his earth-caked hands, he came over to the fire to warm them, rasping them together. He stooped over the blaze Cressy had made, looking sideways up at her.

'Your mother's gone with Kate and poor little Petronella to see Dr O'Connor. In the Rolls-Royce,' he said with solemnity.

'Is something wrong?' Cressy guessed there was, from Pet having been given her full name.

'Not with your mother. God bless you, no. But we're all at sixes and sevens here.'

He pulled at a loose end of wool in the sleeve of his jersey and began to unravel it. Both watched, fascinated.

'Is Pet ill?' Cressy asked.

'It's very much feared she's in the family way, don't you know.'

'How *should* I know?' Sometimes her father's turns of phrase enraged her.

'Well, no, of course,' he said mildly, 'but that's the way it appears to be.'

'But who on earth does she know?'

Her father stopped unravelling the wool, and tried to tuck it inside his sleeve out of sight.

'This is not divulged. Or not to me. Not divulged,' he repeated vaguely, straightening his back and looking about the room. 'Would you like a cup of tea?'

'No, it's too much trouble.'

'A glass of milk then?'

She nodded her head, thinking furiously, but not of what he was saying. Her meek and mild little cousin, who had turned away in contempt when Cressy had told her of the discoveries she had made amongst her grandfather's books. She almost felt that Pet, in her new situation, had stolen a march on her.

She followed her father into the kitchen and rummaged in tins in the larder. There was a new kind of cake she could not remember her mother making, and it seemed strange that they should go on eating meals without her, even making experiments, just to please themselves.

'Has Grandfather had any of those young men about lately in the workshop?' she asked.

'No, no. I thought of that too.' Her father held a glass to her in his grimy hands. They sipped in silence, and Cressy ate a piece of cake, while going over the possibilities – the cousins, Bartholomew and James; but they were schoolboys and always treated aloofly by the three girls. Incest, perhaps; but not her father, Joe, for he had said the name was not divulged to him. She even thought with horror of her grandfather, and of Father Daughtry, of the nasty little man who came up to slaughter the pigs, or the postman, meeting Pet secretly in Quayne Woods, propping his bicycle against the hedge.

'Your mother will be sorry to have missed you,' Joe said.

'I can always come again. Are they going to get married?'

'Who?'

'Why, Pet and this undivulged man?'

'I believe it's not on the cards.'

'Is he married already then?' Or a priest, she wondered.

'When you come next time you shall talk to your mother about it. She will tell you what has to be told. I'm not in the know much. It's more in the women's province.'

Cressy felt that it would be easier to come now. The trouble Pet was in was not as bad as having been married in a registry office; but it was bad enough.

'How is your book going?' she asked politely. She went to fetch her coat, and he took it and held it for her.

'It's coming along nicely now,' he said, as if it were an invalid, and he was pleased to have it inquired after.

'Good. Well, I'd better go. Will you give my love to Mother?'

'I'd walk down with you, but I have to go over and help your grandfather shift some canvases.'

'And what does *he* say about it?' Cressy asked.

Half-way down Quayne Hill, Midge was waiting in the car. She had made it a little den of cigarette smoke, was listening to the six o'clock news, hunched up in her sheepskin coat.

'Jump in,' she said to Cressy, leaning over and opening the door. 'I thought you'd be tired.'

'Oh, you are the most thoughtful woman I ever knew,' Cressy said, getting in. Indeed, Midge did have a great number of thoughts. Few could have more.

'I was at a loose end, anyway,' she said. 'And how are things at Quayne?'

'My father says they are at sixes and sevens, which is a funny way of saying that my cousin, Pet, is pregnant.'

Midge drove slowly, so glad that she had persuaded Cressy to pay her call. The news was better than anything she could have envisaged; for she hated Quayne and all about it, had felt herself patronised there, and thought it had been the most terrible wedding she ever was at.

'And what does your grandfather say about *this*?' she asked, in a voice braced with anticipation.

'Father says that the odd thing is that he is so taken up with a trouble of his own that he scarcely has time to think about poor Pet.'

'A trouble of his own?' It was getting better and better, Midge thought. Perhaps the rot of all time was setting in. She sincerely hoped so.

'They are cutting down Quayne Woods to build six Regency houses there.'

'You can't build Regency houses at this time of history.'

'Type.'

'I thought the woods belonged to him.'

'To the Castle. And they are getting hard up there.'

The Castle was miles away. Quayne was once one of its farms. Selling it to Harry had been the first of the measures against death duties. Other measures had followed. They had opened the place for half-crowns, but there was nothing to see inside, but damp stone floors, black, almost faceless portraits, and threadbare carpets: no one was interested, felt nothing but pity or contempt. Then timber had been felled; now, to more purpose, to make room for Regency-type houses for commuters.

'I can't see that that's too bad for him,' Midge said, disappointed. 'Shall we have a quick one at the Horseshoes? Or must you hurry back to cook dinner?'

'It's only bangers,' Cressy said.

CHAPTER ELEVEN

Just as branches were beginning to bud, there was a spell of bad weather. Snow came heavily. Midge's garden was gradually pillowed and bolstered. There were miniature nursery-slopes in the angles of walls, and trees with borne down branches holding an unaccustomed weight.

At the window for long periods, watching the birds making arrowed tracks across the snow to scraps of bread, she could imagine the predicament of everything in the garden, of the trees especially. I have been snowed upon myself, she thought.

From all the whiteness of outside, her drawing-room was brilliantly coloured, and two-dimensional – a painting by Matisse.

The snow isolated her – deep on the paths, and in a drift against the garage door. An occasional red-faced, mufflered tradesman drove along the lane, churning up gravelly slush, and plodded to the back door, leaving a bottle of milk, which sank inches into the snow on the step, or cold parcels of groceries. To find the damp newspaper stuck in the letter-box was the high point of the day. Mrs Brindle did not arrive.

The house, for all its brilliant colours, was dead. There

seemed nothing to hope for between getting up and going to bed.

Cressy was worse off across her field; for pipes froze and the telephone wire had come down; but the television worked, and she had her little store of beans and sardines, so her life was not too much disrupted. More than ever, David cursed the country, and having to come home to it at night, and even when he had reached it, having to shovel snow and try to unfreeze the pipes. Driving home at night, he had disloyal thoughts about Cressy, marvelling at his madness in marrying her. He loved her – especially for bringing out in him a tenderness he had never felt before; but she cost him a good deal in comfort. The only meals he enjoyed now were those at his mother's house. As she was so willing to invite them, and both of them so eager to go, they were there more and more often. ('Can't you teach Cressy to make this?' he had once asked. 'I'm not that sort of mother-in-law,' Midge had said primly. 'I could never learn, anyway,' Cressy said.) Midge thought that for her the old saying was half untrue – she had lost a son, and gained a daughter. It was a novelty to her.

David's comfort was gone, and he mourned it: and responsibility had come, and irked him. Like a child, Cressy both exasperated him and endeared herself to him. If only we could live in London, everything would be all right, he told himself, for the hundredth time, driving home one particularly dreadful night, with snowflakes swirling towards his headlights and clotting on the windscreen. The wipers moved slowly, then jammed. He got out of the car and stepped into a foot of soft snow. He began to think of a base plan for staying the next night in London, inventing excuses. She can go to Mother's he decided. For the duration. (Of the snow, he meant.) He cleared the windscreen and drove on, his socks sopping wet as the snow on them melted. He dreamed of civilisation – he and Nell dining at the White Tower, perhaps; or chop-sticking somewhere.

At the Three Horseshoes, he stopped for a drink and a warm by the fire before facing the day's disaster at home. Quayne was cut off from the village, so Joe MacPhail and the Father must have been forced to drink parsnip wine at home. No one was about. The saloon bar was empty.

'Surprise, surprise!' the barmaid said, perking up as he entered. 'And what is your pleasure, kind sir?'

'I'll have a pint of the usual.'

She pulled on the beer pump, and the bitter swelled up in the glass and, as he watched it, watching her, up swelled his own misery, keeping level with the beer until, like that, it threatened to spill over. Her arm muscles moved, and there was a movement of her breast, as she drew on the lever. She was conscious, he knew, of the sexuality of this.

He took his beer to the imitation log-fire and tried to warm one foot, then the other. 'Stepped into a great snow-drift,' he explained.

'Did you, darling?' she asked, with professional sympathy, hardly listening, but looking at his cross and handsome face. 'How's the wife?' she asked.

'She's well, thank you.'

'I hear that poor little cousin of hers up at Quayne is in the club. So it goes in the village.'

So it does, does it! David thought. 'I'll have a large Scotch,' he said, putting down his empty glass.

'And so you shall, dear.' She reached up to the optic, with the same display of bosom movement. The door opened and, to David's relief, Toby came in.

'Stepped in a snow-drift,' David said, putting down the money for his drink and Toby's.

'I thought you looked sorry for yourself. I must say I'm bloody glad *I* don't have to go out to work. Can you find such a thing in the pub as a bottle of Burgundy?' he asked the barmaid.

'Might do,' she said, taking a bunch of keys from the hook.

'We've a great winter's night stew going on,' Toby said.

'Lucky sod.' David had gone back to the fire, and moodily held out one faintly steaming shoe.

'Well, you're more than welcome,' Toby said. 'It's in a casserole the size of a cauldron. But I suppose Cressy has something waiting.'

'You know you suppose nothing of the kind.'

Toby looked uneasy. Come to think of it, he could not imagine Cressy, with the best will in the world, accomplishing anything; but there was no need for David to be sour with him about it. He had not made him marry her.

The barmaid came back from the cellar with a bottle misted with cold, and Toby set it down by the fire. 'Give her a ring,' he said, meaning Cressy.

'The telephone's packed up.'

'Well . . . as I say . . . come and warm your feet for a minute and have a drink with Alexia.'

'That's right, make off with my one and only customer,' the barmaid complained. 'What have I done, I'd like to know.'

'I mustn't stay a moment,' David said. The temptation not to go home, in spite of Cressy, was too great. With the bottle inside his coat, Toby said good night to the barmaid, and led the way.

The room at the back of the shop was beautifully warm. There was a rich smell of meat and cloves and bay-leaves cooking, and Alexia fetched a pair of socks, and stuffed his wet shoes with newspaper and put them near the fire to dry.

'I've still got to get through the snow to the cottage,' David said, drinking some more whisky and, apart from the prospect before him, feeling much better.

'But you'll start off warm,' she said.

She's so beautiful, he thought, watching her. Beautiful jaw; beautiful cheek-bones; beautiful movements – and none consciously made.

Before long, he was sitting with them at the table, and Alexia was ladling out meat from the casserole on to his plate.

'I don't know how you face that awful drive down from London day after day,' Toby said.

'If it weren't for my mother, I wouldn't.'

'You should make her go to live in London, too, Alexia said.

'She loves her home here.'

'Her having it both ways is at a pretty great cost to you, isn't it?' Alexia said. 'My God, Toby, this wine is freezing,' she added, obviously not wanting David's answer, having made her point.

When at last he reached home, Cressy had gone to bed. On the table in the kitchen was a dish covered with some blackened pastry. He felt muzzy from the wine and whisky, and he peered closely at it, but came to no conclusion. He poured out another drink and, when he had finished it, went upstairs.

Cressy was sitting up in bed, with the light on, wearing one of his sweaters against the cold. She began to cry as soon as she saw him. He thought of bolting downstairs to get another drink. I can't go through it, he told himself, thinking of the crying bout ahead. Too tired, too cold, too bored.

'I thought you were dead,' she said. 'I'm only crying from relief.'

'Why should I be dead? I happened to meet Toby. I'd just walked into about three feet of snow, I'd have you know. How would you like that?'

'Your supper got spoiled.'

'Yes, I saw something peculiar down there.'

'And I particularly wanted it to be nice for you.'

'Quite a change of heart,' he said heavily, sitting down on the edge of the bed with his back to her, taking off his shoes.

'What do you mean "a change of heart"?'

'Only that if I'd known you were actually cooking something, I'd have come home earlier.'

'And I had my news to tell you.'

He waited for it indifferently, tugged at a shoe and threw it across the floor.

'Your mother came here this morning – all through that snow, just to bring me some cakes.'

'Really! That news I don't find very exciting.'

'But I haven't told you yet. Your mother thinks I am going to have a baby.'

He turned round to stare at her. 'What do you mean, my mother thinks you are going to have a baby?'

'I was being sick when she came.'

She pulled the neck of his sweater up round her chin, and shivered, staring back at his astonished face.

'But you've taken your pills, haven't you?'

'Yes, of course. I've hardly missed a single day. Don't you *want* a baby? Your mother was so pleased by the idea, and I thought you would be. She said she'd never really had the chance to be a grandmother – with the others so far away.'

'What my mother wants is beside the point. If *we* wanted a child, why in God's name take the pills at all? You are completely feckless,' he said furiously.

'Oh, don't be angry,' she pleaded. 'Don't be angry with me.'

He began to undress. 'Look, I'm tired,' he explained wearily. 'I'm cold. I've had a bloody awful day, and now you face me with this. I've got just about enough on my plate at present – without babies.'

'And I've had a bloody awful day, too,' Cressy said, weeping loudly. 'Hour after hour on my own, and the television's gone

123

wrong. It was snowing on that, too. I'm afraid the hot-waterbottle's gone cold,' she said timidly, as he threw back the bedclothes and let in a draught.

'And my feet are like ice.' With an exaggerated air of patience, he replaced the bedclothes, put on his dressing-gown and slippers, took the cold bottle and went downstairs. He filled the kettle and refilled his glass and stood by the stove, drinking. In no time at all, it would be the black and silent morning, the beginning of another dreadful day, with new tracks of little animals on the freshly fallen snow when it was light enough to see them, waste-pipes frozen, trouble with the car. He ruffled his hair tiredly, drained his glass, waiting for the kettle to boil.

CHAPTER TWELVE

In this weather, Aunt Sylvie died. It was as Archie had foretold. She simply diminished and faded away. He watched her going, with great sadness.

David went to the funeral, drove with his father behind the hearse, through the grey, town slush. A few black figures walked between the snow-laden bushes up the path to the church. From the religion she had not believed in was borrowed the final tidying-up. Archie could think of no other seemly kind of send-off, and she had left no instructions, apart from those – mostly impossible to carry out – for the disposal of her belongings.

Standing in the cemetery, David wondered how they had managed to dig the grave – the ground was like iron. Even the mauve and white chrysanthemums looked nipped with cold. He worried about his father, standing there shivering, his eyes watering.

They drove back to the house.

'Shouldn't we have asked the Vicar for a cuppa, or a drink or something?' David asked.

'Never took to the fellow. He was poor Sylvie's sparring-partner. Shan't be seeing much more of *him*.'

Who will he be seeing much more of, David wondered, as they went into the dark and ugly house.

'Can't say I'm not a bit cut-up,' Archie said, looking about the hall, feeling very strange about the emptiness of upstairs.

'Shall I make *you* a cuppa?' David asked.

His father winced. 'Let us have a glass of something,' he suggested. 'We need to drive out the cold.'

'We do indeed.'

Archie brought the decanter of port and the biscuit-barrel from the sideboard in the dining-room, and they settled by the oil-heater in the drawing-room, Archie with his rug about his knees.

'Father,' David began nervously, 'you simply can't go on living here alone. You've done one duty; now what about the other?'

'I have no other, dear boy. My great, grown-up sons can look after themselves. And very well they seem to do it. Most proud.'

'You have a very lonely wife. She has to face old age on her own. As *you* will have to now.'

Archie made secretive, crumbling movements of his fingers about his nostrils. 'But she's got you to hand,' he said slyly. 'And that young girl of yours. Seems to have worked out very well.'

'But, dammit, I can't take a husband's place. And why should I have to try?'

'She wouldn't want me back, would she?' Craftily, Archie watched David's face. 'I wasn't much of a success, you know.'

'We could soon find out.'

'No, I simply couldn't stand the pace. I couldn't then, and now it's out of the question. Here, there, and everywhere, and all at the same time, it seemed to me. I remember that once I had to go to the Golf Club Dance. Imagine it. Does she still go dancing?'

'No,' said David, 'for there is no one to take her. I am a little ashamed that I do not.'

'Oh, you'd enjoy it, I'm sure.'

'In any case,' David said hastily, 'she no longer cares for such things.'

Archie was silent to express his disbelief.

'But what will you do here, all on your own?' David asked him.

'Oh, I am always on the go. I do my housework, when Mrs Thingummy doesn't turn up, and I cook luncheon. Then a little snooze, I must confess, and after tea I do the crossword-puzzle, unless it is one of my silver evenings. And by then, it's time to change for dinner . . .'

He was like a very bad repertory actor in the part of an old man, David thought – the quavering voice and wavering gestures. One of the many lines across his forehead might be the join of an almost bald wig.

'And you could live in comfort, and be looked after and eat delicious food.'

There was a little cackle. 'Sarcasm is held to be the lowest form of wit, but I must say I always enjoy it,' Archie said. 'No, I am very well as I am, and I think you know it.'

David refilled their glasses, and took another stale, soft biscuit. It tasted of sadness, appropriate to the day, and the surroundings.

'Cressy, my wife, is expecting a baby,' he said.

'Poor little boy,' said Archie.

The thaw began the day after the funeral. Great shelves of snow came crashing down from Midge's roof, and drops off branches pitted the melting snow. With the thaw, Mrs Brindle came again, but too full of news to do much work.

'I was sorry to hear about the little cousin up at Quayne,' she lied. 'I wouldn't have mentioned it, but it's all round the village now. You know what villages are like.'

During the bad weather, she could not go up to Quayne, so had busied herself in other ways.

The village was inimical to Quayne, and had in general received the story gladly: even usually charitable people forgave themselves easily for caring less than they should about another's unhappiness, for self-sufficiency is an irritating thing in a small village, where giving and taking is the accepted order. Quayne did not even give its custom to the shopkeepers – could manage largely without them, it seemed – took no part in anything, did not even go to church. Joe MacPhail's and Father Daughtry's visits to the pub were all the village saw of Quayne money, and as often as not, they put their drinks on the slate.

'And they're supposed to be better than us,' Mrs Brindle had said over and over again in the last few days, and said it once more, this morning of the thaw, to Midge.

'They only supposed it themselves,' Midge replied.

'And that chap – what's his name – I couldn't ever stand him. He could be her father, and even then too old. A married man, they say, though I never set eyes on any wife.'

Mrs Brindle knew more than Midge, but Midge could hardly ask questions. Mrs Brindle sensed this, and changed the subject, enjoying herself. 'You've had a fox up the drive, I see,' she said.

'They must be starving.'

'Who brought all those logs in? Surely you never carried that lot?'

'My son came up at the week-end to see if I was all right. And got stuck in the snow for his trouble.'

'I expect *she's* put out.'

'Who?'

'His wife. About her cousin.'

'I suppose so. Everybody must be. It's not a very good start in life for a child – and she has hardly started her own life, poor girl.'

'And can't marry the man, it seems. They don't believe in divorce, you see.'

'He's a Roman Catholic, too.' Midge's voice did not betray whether this were a statement or a question.

'Who goes up there who isn't? Bar me. Not that it would make any difference what he was. I mean, her grandfather wouldn't stand for her getting married to anyone divorced.'

'It isn't her grandfather who made that rule.'

'Then it's one of the few he hasn't.'

Over her elevenses, Mrs Brindle relented. 'I can't help wondering,' she said, 'whether we'll be seeing so much of Mr Leofric Welland from now on. And what a name that is to be blessed with. No, I wonder very much. I must say my blood ran cold at one of the conversations I had no means of not over-hearing. The girl was crying – they're great for floods of tears up there – and she said to him, to her grandfather, "I never want to see him again as long as I live." This was in the kitchen where they were having a bit of a *tête-à-tête* and taking not a blind bit of notice of me in the scullery. Clattering about with the dishes, I was, and coughing my head off. "But there must have been some love between you," he said – or words to that effect. "And, in any case," he said, "Leofric has his work to do here. His life work. That's important, too." He's writing a book, you know, that one. They're all in it. But his lordship most of all, as you may guess. You've never read such twaddle.'

Midge did not have to wonder how Mrs Brindle had.

'Well, really, it's no concern of mine,' she said at last. 'I'm afraid I've rather let the brass go while you've been away.'

'I'll give it a going-over when I've washed up these few

things,' Mrs Brindle said, making a little bustle of getting up from her chair.

In the afternoon, after Mrs Brindle had gone, David unexpectedly arrived.

'So good to be warm,' he said, crouching by the fire.

'You've got a streaming cold,' Midge said. 'You shouldn't have come out.'

'That's *why* I came out. Now the kitchen's half-flooded. It's coming through the roof, all over the place, and we've put down every basin and bucket we possess to catch it. We had to move the bed. There was a nice little trickle into that too. I couldn't possibly have gone to work and left Cressy to deal with it. I wondered if it would put you out too much if we came here for tonight, until I can get something done about the roof and dry the mattress.'

'But, of course, it doesn't put me out. You can come for as long as you like.'

'I thought you wouldn't mind.'

'I am delighted.'

'Then I'll go and fetch Cressy. She'll be delighted, too. She's a bit under the weather. Yes, literally.'

'I thought so.'

He made no move to get up.

'How did the funeral go?' Midge asked.

'You can imagine. Simply terrible. I went back with him afterwards to that awful house – hated leaving him there alone. It all seems so damned stupid to me – *both* of you on your own.'

Midge said nothing.

'If he wanted to – would you have him back?'

'He wouldn't want to.'

'Oh, well, I still think it's bloody nonsensical. By the way, Cressy tells me you think she's pregnant.'

'The girls at Quayne seem to have a certain vagueness in common.'

'It's too bad,' he complained, turning his handkerchief about, trying to find a dry bit to blow his nose into.

'I hope you haven't said as much to Cressy.'

'Well, I did, I'm afraid. I had too much to drink last night with Toby and Alexia, and I was at the end of my tether, this cold coming on. Today, Cressy keeps crying. You know how she does. It gets me down.'

'It used not to.'

'Well, at the moment, it just makes me want to clout her.'

'Then I'm ashamed of you. Go back home and fetch her, and jolly well tell her how pleased you really are. I'm going to put the fire on in your bedroom, and I shall insist you have an early night. What about a supper-tray in bed?'

'Bliss,' he said, getting up wearily. 'Right, I'll go now. I shan't be able to get back home fast enough.'

She wondered which house he meant when he said 'home'. As soon as he had gone, she ran up the stairs, as lightly as a young girl.

Later in the evening, when David was in bed, Midge and Cressy sat by the fire.

'He can be a bit sulky,' Midge said. 'One has to face that. But he confessed he was absolutely stoned last night, and didn't really know what he was saying.'

'He wouldn't speak to me when he came to bed. It was our first quarrel.'

'I think he was very naughty.'

'Did you quarrel with *your* husband . . . well, of course, I suppose so . . . ending the way it did.'

'Alas! he was not the quarrelling sort. He seemed to have no emotions. He would never have gone beyond being irritable –

just slightly irritable, that was his prevailing mood, and a little depressed always. I suppose my fault. And he had stomach ulcers. Nothing but invalid food. I expect I was to blame for that, too. But to live with someone who is always on one level, as I did all those years, is deadly. A really maddening thing I remember was hearing him chuckling to himself in his sleep one night – for he hardly ever laughed. What the hell's he laughing at? I wondered, and I knew I'd never know. He got the better of me there.'

'It sounds as if you are well rid of him,' Cressy said, forgetting to play the game as David had instructed.

CHAPTER THIRTEEN

'When I remember what she went through,' David was saying to Nell, in a city pub. 'Escaping from home, from a complete system, I so much admired her energy and gallantry. She was up against all of her world. And was only a child.'

'"Gallantry" is *such* a word,' Nell said, looking about her at all the dark-suited men. She had hauled herself up on to a high stool by the bar, and her skirt was rucked up. David glanced at it, thought of telling her, but could not be bothered.

'Character is something. I admired that in her, not having much myself,' he said.

'I wouldn't say that,' Nell remarked vaguely. 'Aren't these men dreadful?'

'All congregations of men are absurd,' David said, 'except, I suppose, on battlefields.'

'Gallantry again,' Nell murmured. 'But I don't know much about battlefields.'

'Nor I. Only domestic ones.'

'And I dare say all collections of women are ridiculous. We were meant to offset one another. Do you mind!' she said sharply, to a man on her other side who had jogged her elbow.

She kept her eyes on them, listening to that little party, not to David.

'It's himself!' was said, to the pushing newcomer. 'What will you be after having, Stan? The Worthington's off. We're Doubling the Diamond.'

'I'll do this.'

'No, it's my shout.'

'We were going out to dinner with Toby and Alexia,' David went on, and Nell turned her head, resigning herself to him. She thought he was simply the limit, leading her, all that time, to believe he wanted to marry her, then asking someone else, and now boring her with his complaints.

'I got home a bit late because of the traffic, and there she was sitting by the fire in her dressing-gown.'

Nell rustled about in her large handbag, and took out a ten-shilling note.

'I'll do this,' David said.

'No, it's my shout as *they* say.' And she did, in fact, lean over the bar and shout to the Irish barman, who had the narrow, pale, girlish face of a Picasso harlequin. He looked alarmed, darted towards the whisky optic, his tongue between his lips, his brows drawn together – newly arrived on English soil, she surmised.

'Yes, the dressing-gown,' she prompted David patiently, turning to him again.

'Well, I thought she was ready – all but her dress – and I rushed upstairs and washed and tore around for all I was worth.'

'And then?'

'When I went downstairs, she was still sitting there, having a drink with my mother.'

'Was she going out with you – Midge?'

'No.'

'Oh, I see.'

David paused, then took a sip from his glass. 'She hadn't even begun to get ready, and had had all day to do it.'

'So you had a good old set-to.'

'I'm afraid we did.'

'And what did your mother do about that?'

'She got up and went into the kitchen.'

'Ah yes, having no part in it.'

'What do you mean "ah yes!"?'

'Having started it, then having, as I say, no part in it. Why, in heaven's name, didn't she tell Cressy to get a move on, instead of giving her a drink?'

As David made no reply, she let her attention wander again. 'They're talking about the insides of cars now,' she told him. 'Nothing bores me more.'

'They're not out to entertain *you*.'

The sandwiches they had ordered were now put in front of them, and Nell lifted a corner of one of hers and peered short-sightedly inside – hard-boiled egg, sliced, with dark rings round the yolk, a scattering of cress, black seeds as well.

'The reason, they say, that women novelists can't write about men, is because they don't know what they're like when they're alone together, what they talk about and so on. But I can't think why they don't know. I seem to hear them booming away all the time. Just listen to this lot, next to me.'

'Awful bread,' David said. 'It feels damp. Cressy used to buy this when we were at home.'

'Well, I should care,' Nell said. 'I get it wherever I go. How long will you be staying under your mother's roof?'

'Until our own is mended.'

'The devil of a time it's been.'

'You don't know what it's like in the country. They come and go. They're undertakers as well, so every time there's a funeral they knock off and get into their mute's rig-out. And at this time of the year, people are dying right and left, as you may suppose, after all that weather. Apart from that, every time anything goes wrong with the church, the Vicar has them at his beck and call. Priority. You simply don't know what a village can be like.'

'Oh, yes, I do. Would you believe it, they're talking about Gay Paree now. What they paid for everything, and was it worth it: no, I'll say it wasn't. Rooked, fleeced, taken for a ride. Cold plates, raw lamb, sour cream, had to peel their own shrimps.' Then, altering her tone, turning to cut off the other conversation and give him her whole attention, she said, 'I seriously think, darling, that you'll have to get out. Why don't you bring Cressy up to London for a bit? You can kip down with me. I've got a spare bed and a sofa. Make a break for you both.'

'You're a dear, generous girl, but I simply couldn't do it. My mother's a bundle of nerves when she's alone at night. I once came in unexpectedly and found her in a terrible state.'

'She didn't know you were coming?'

'No, she didn't,' he snapped. 'It's bad enough for her being on her own, even when she knows that we're near by. She sleeps with the telephone on the bed, and all the lights on.'

Nell looked at the ceiling. Then she said, 'I only thought it might help your marriage. But please yourself.'

'Cressy and her cravings,' Midge explained to David, bringing to the table a bread and butter pudding smothered with nutmeg.

David had at first been amused by the cravings, and had himself gone to some trouble in London to buy lychees; but, by now, he was irritated by the number, the variety of the idiosyncrasies – there seemed to be a new one every day. Any stray fancy that came into her head at once became a craving, something she would even walk to the village to buy – liquorice

136

allsorts, tinned grapefruit, black treacle: nothing very expensive, like strawberries out of season, for she was an unspoilt, undemanding girl – but oddities, and eccentricities. Various smells were the most compelling fancies of all. Entranced, she hovered by a newly-creosoted fence, used eucalyptus-oil instead of scent, merely for the pleasure of having it on her clothes. She even went down to the village and bought herself a quarter of a pound of camphor balls, like a child buying sweets. Now this nutmeg, the latest of the whims. All were smells David could no more abide than the bread and butter pudding.

'No, thank you,' he said sternly, as the spoon went into the dish for his helping.

Cressy bent her head over the plate and, with closed eyes, breathed in the spicy smell. Sniffing and nibbling, sniffing and nibbling, David said to himself over and over again, to while away the time until they had finished. Until he could get down, he thought; for the two women ate calmly, ignoring him, as if he were a child who had made a fuss.

He put his napkin on the table, and turned slightly to look out of the window.

'Have some cheese afterwards,' Midge suggested. 'Afterwards' obviously meant 'when *we* have finished our delicious pudding'.

He had, of course, confided in Nell about the cravings, and how they were getting on his nerves, and she had said that there could not be any physical reason for them, as far as she were able to see; unless a sharpening of the senses, which could hardly account for the tinned grapefruit. 'But why ask me?' she in her turn had asked. 'I'm just an old maid.'

'A very wise old maid,' David had said. He had meant to imply that her wisdom lay in being unmarried, but she had narrowed her eyes, and muttered the words after him. '"A very wise old maid", is it? I think, my boy, that you can do your morose drinking with someone else from now on.'

So he was out with everyone, for the first time in his life.

He stirred; he sighed; *they* had a second helping.

'Sorry if we're keeping you,' Midge said sarcastically, in a tone she had not used since Archie went, and David could not remember ever having heard.

Pet, unlike her cousin, was too proud to allow herself cravings. For they would only have drawn attention to her plight. Now her days seemed dull and never-ending. Listlessly, she sat for Harry, or, rather, stood for him. As far as he was concerned, her plight had come at the right time. Before her pregnancy showed, he had painted her as the Virgin Mary entering the house of Zacharias. She stood in the doorway, wearing a home-spun skirt and a fairisle sweater, her hair falling to her shoulders. Her head was haloed. These days, she was posing for the other half of the picture – the pregnant Elizabeth, just risen from a chair in greeting, one hand on the table, the other on her belly, some knitting fallen from her lap to the floor.

Pet and Cressy stood before the unfinished painting in the studio. Harry had gone to London to give a lecture, and they were safe and alone in there, alone for the first time since Cressy had left Quayne.

'That was Gabriel's busy time,' Cressy remarked, looking up at the picture.

Everything in the living-room of Zacharias's house was slant-ing and broken up – a mad aspidistra, refracted light streaming over Mary from the open door, a crooked window covered with lace curtains, bric-à-brac everywhere, an old woman's room.

'It always takes me such ages to sort out what everything is,' Cressy complained. 'I can't see the point in his making it so dif-ficult. And he does it more and more.'

'Don't you want something to get your teeth into?' Pet asked, and Cressy turned to look at her in surprise at the mocking tone of her voice. 'All of the arts are the same, and he is a *prose* painter,' Pet went on languidly, as one who quotes a boring but well-learned lesson. 'The worst thing a prose *writer* can do is to lapse into poetry, and when he does, if he has any nous, he fractures it, makes something more exciting of it. Trips one's attention.'

They both knew that their grandfather knew all about writing, as well as painting; but Cressy said, 'I can't see the sense in fracturing an aspidistra. It doesn't make it at all exciting to me. And why are you clutching your stomach like that, and with such a look of horror on your face?'

'It is a look of ecstasy, my dear. The child has just quickened in her womb.'

'In, I remember, the sixth month – and not a minute too soon, I should think.'

'Well, she was an old woman. Perhaps that makes a difference. I don't know.'

'At least he's made sure of a family likeness.'

Pet began to laugh, for the first time since her plight began, and Cressy turned to her with a pleased look. The cousins had come together, as in the picture.

Mo, from a window, watched the cousins crossing the courtyard. She decided that, together, they looked absurd, both with their rounded stomachs going before; but, alone, they would not have done. She had a curious sensation, watching them, of recoil, of separation, an intense loneliness, fringed with envy. It had always been, with the three of them, that one was a little left out: usually, it had been Cressy, from her recalcitrance; and now it was she, from her virginity.

'Perhaps she will die,' Cressy said – meaning Leofric's wife – as they walked down the hill, Pet chumming her on her way a little.

'I don't care if she dies or not. I never wish to see him again.'

'I can't think how it ever happened in that case.'

'And no more can I,' Pet said, like an angry child. 'You know what it's like here,' she went on, as if she were at last going to try to explain. 'Prison can't be much worse, can it? I can imagine prisoners doing strange things, just to pass the time, even. We used to go for walks. Surely everyone knew that? He talked to me as if I were a person – a grown-up person, too. He asked me questions about myself.'

'I bet he did.'

'We all like that, I suppose. He always called me Petronella, and even that made me feel different. "Your names are three sweet symphonies," he said. You know – *The Blessed Damozel.*'

'Oh, her!'

'He's written that in his book.'

'How *can* he go on writing about us after this has happened? What a cheek!'

'You're so lucky,' Pet said. 'Though once I thought that you were mad.'

Cressy guessed that she was in danger of being smug about her love for David. In Pet's company, she scarcely allowed herself to think of it – of her miraculous escape, her wonderful new life. She tried to keep her thoughts on her cousin. 'How often did it happen – you and Leofric?' she inquired.

'Only once, thank you very much.'

'I should have thought it hardly possible.'

Pet said nothing, knowing so well that it was.

'Poor Pet.'

'Oh, don't say "poor Pet" again. Everyone has said it over and over. I'd rather they were angry. Who wants to be pathetic?'

Cressy, in her absent-minded way, had been thinking, 'Such a predicament, for such a little sex' – not really of the predicament itself; but she could not say so.

They stopped near the top of the hill to look at the building site – one or two houses with walls quite high already.

'Aren't they awful,' Pet said dutifully.

'Don't be brain-washed. I think they might look very nice. And perhaps some nice people will come to live in them. It might be the beginning of something different for you.'

'Not for me,' Pet said bitterly. Suddenly, she put her cold hands to her cheeks. 'Oh, what shall I do? What *shall* I do?'

She shall share *my* happiness, Cressy determined. There is so much of it. I must find a way of letting it spill over.

Pet had recovered. 'I don't think I'll come any farther,' she said. 'I get so puffed climbing hills.' Before she turned away, she glanced again at the building. 'I still think they're ghastly,' she said.

CHAPTER FOURTEEN

I can't think why birds don't get duodenal ulcers,' Midge said to Mrs Brindle. She was standing at one of the drawing-room windows, watching them, her birds, swooping into and away from the ham-bone on the lawn. 'It's terrible the way they have to eat their food, so full of anxiety all the time.'

'Perhaps they do get them, ulcers,' Mrs Brindle said, flicking her duster along bookshelves. 'We're hardly to know.'

The ham-bone was left over from David's and Cressy's stay. Mrs Brindle thought she could have made a little pie with the meat left on it, but it was already out on the lawn before she arrived.

'There are some kidneys in the fridge if you'd like to take them home,' Midge said, as if she had read her thoughts. 'I meant them for breakfast yesterday, but they only wanted bacon and sausages.'

During the long visit, she had over-catered, and wildly so towards the end. The previous day Cressy had gone back to the cottage laden. She had, also, Midge was pleased to think, gone home reluctantly.

Midge had spent the day with her, getting everything ready

for David's return in the evening. His contentment there had to be assured.

'You must stay and have some supper with us,' Cressy had said. 'I insist on it. We shall never manage to finish up this meat on our own. And that great wedge of Brie will run out of its sides before we can eat it all.'

But despite all they had done, David had not seemed to marvel at the results when he came back. And Midge had returned home depressed, to lie in bed and go through a conversation she had overheard a night or two before, across the landing, from their bedroom, David's voice distinct with exasperation. 'Let's face the fact,' he had said. 'We'll never make anything of it.'

Of what? Midge wondered fearfully. Of their marriage? Their future? It was difficult to tell for Cressy was weeping softly.

'I'm *not* angry with you,' David said. 'But I *am* very angry with myself. I've behaved like a fool, as Nell pointed out.'

'I'm tired of hearing about Nell,' Cressy said, with a little gust of anger.

'O.K. But I've come to see that she is right. Whatever you think about her, she has always had plenty of common sense.'

'But *can* you have a baby in a flat in London?'

'I have plenty of friends who do.'

'Well, you know I don't care where I am as long as I'm with you. Anyone would think it was me who said we had to stay here.'

Perhaps he had corrected her grammar, for she burst out, 'Oh, I know I'm just an ignorant child. I can't think why you ever married me. I knew you'd get fed up. It was too good to be true.'

There were vague, soothing noises. 'It's because everything here gets on my nerves,' David said presently. Cressy asked, 'But what about your mother?'

And then he lowered his voice, remembering, obviously, where he was and who might over-hear him. Midge, straining to hear her fate, heard nothing.

She stood in her room, very still, her hands frozen. Murmuring continued for a time from across the landing, and Cressy seemed to have cheered up; she even laughed, and Midge heard her say, 'As long as you'll be better-tempered. I can't bear it when you're cross,' and then, 'which bed shall I get into, yours or mine?'

Midge very softly closed her bedroom door. She should have given up her own bed, she thought, but she would never have been able to make the suggestion. Usually, when she had taken in their early-morning tea, they had been lying in one of the single beds in the spare room, and she had kept her eyes carefully on the tray, and had been brisk about where to set it down, feeling for some reason embarrassed.

That night of the conversation, she had hardly slept at all. She determined to put all her energies into beautifying the cottage, and so make it dear to both of them. All that day when Cressy moved back, she had worked hard to banish David's disenchantment; but she guessed that her labours had had very little effect. He was growing more and more like his father, and seemed to come home always nowadays in a state of suppressed irritation.

She knew that so much driving through that hard winter had worn him out; but the summer was coming, and the long, light evenings. She thought hopefully of that, and not beyond. He had had bad weather when he was living with her, but had at least come home to comfort, a good meal, no domestic crises, no responsibilities. He is a bachelor at heart, she told herself angrily. He should have had the sense to remain one.

The threat of their going away was with her all the time now, and this morning, disconsolately watching the birds, she wondered how she could make herself ready to meet it.

'There!' said Mrs Brindle, glancing round the room to see if any speck of dust remained.

Midge turned from the window. Her sudden movement made all the birds on the lawn fly up and away. Indeed, the room looked very beautiful, so burnished and colourful. Mrs Brindle seemed satisfied with it, and left Midge on her own to admire her work.

But Midge was putting the room in the balance. The price of it – of all her lovely things – was her loneliness. That was the threat. It was even more than loneliness, which might be of such a kind that Mrs Brindle's mornings would become the high spots of the week. It was also her terror at night, and her despair on waking. A long emptiness before her, and all the days the same. And her grandchild snatched away from her – as she had been deprived of the others. Short visits would only bring a stranger. She had looked forward to a day-to-day life with the child.

Some tulip petals – as if having waited for Mrs Brindle to finish her work – slithered softly on to a table. She scooped them up in her hand, dusting away the pollen, thinking that they had lasted the visit out. It seemed hardly worth doing flowers for herself – as it seemed hardly worth dressing in the morning, or wearing make-up; but not doing these things, she told herself sternly, would diminish all she was to pay for so dearly – the order of her surroundings, all she had created since Archie went away. She determined to go out into the garden and pick a great basketful of flowers and sprays of blossom. But, instead, she walked up and down the room with the soft tulip petals in her hand, crushed them till they were pulp, then threw them with disgust upon the fire. Her breathing was wavering, from her great tension. At least I am forewarned, she told

145

herself, her lips moving, as in the old days when she was alone all day, before the joy of having Cressy in the house.

She started when Mrs Brindle opened the door suddenly.

'Baker, madam.'

'No bread,' Midge said dully.

On Saturday morning, the telephone rang – the first time for some days. During those days, Midge had sometimes had conversations with herself, on the lines of the correspondence pages in some women's magazines – the self-pitying letter, and the brisk, abrasive reply. If she could take an interest in other people, she told herself, she might feel a great deal better. Was there not more than enough for a woman in her position to do? Meals on wheels – going round the cottages with hot dinners and a cheery smile for the old souls. But she disliked old people and would never be able to find a cheery smile for them.

Often she felt exhausted, as if at the end of a long and searching interview, the words going on and on in her mind. And even if I fill my days, she thought, the nights remain.

She crossed the hall that Saturday morning and took up the receiver. David said, 'We're just going to the pub. Cressy thought you might like to come, too.'

A nice way of putting it, Midge thought. The tactful son. But perhaps it had been that way. 'She may be missing us,' Cressy may have said.

'I'd like nothing more,' Midge replied, 'but this morning, I'm afraid I don't feel up to it.'

David thought that her voice sounded frail and strained. 'Is something wrong?' he asked. 'Are you ill?'

'Of course not, darling; but just not in a mood for company.'

'What is it?' He sounded concerned, she thought.

'My back's a bit groggy. Nothing to worry about. It's come and gone before, heaven knows.'

'*I didn't know.*'

'Anno Domini, old boy. Nothing to worry about,' she said again.

'Is there anything I can do?'

'Of course not, darling. I'm perfectly all right with you just down the road. I know that if I need you, I can give you a ring.'

'We'll look in some time.'

'Well, I'd love to see you, but I'm sure you've got plenty to do. Just to know you're there is enough.'

'No, of course, we'll come.'

'I'll say good-bye now. Thank you for asking me.'

She hung up the receiver, and went slowly back to the drawing-room, walking stiffly, warily, easing herself into an armchair as if she were an old woman, putting her hand to her forehead, shutting her eyes.

In the Three Horseshoes it was bright and noisy. Wives came in to join their husbands after shopping; dogs sniffed about the floor for bits of potato crisps, and children, in cars outside, were handed out bottles of Coca-Cola and straws. There was great bonhomie in the atmosphere, the relaxation of Saturday morning, and the anticipation of leisure.

'Well, you're coming along nicely,' Father Daughtry said to Cressy, looking her over – as if she were some old peasant woman from the bog, as Alexia said to her brother.

Cressy was already enormous. Her skirt went up in an arc above her knees, dipped at the back, and was fastened at the waist, David knew, by a chain of safety-pins. She had a bag of potato crisps and was shaking salt into it. She never stopped eating. Sometimes in the night he heard her creeping out of bed and downstairs to find herself a piece of cake. She had become completely torpid, and never walked anywhere. Quayne Hill was out of the question. She hadn't the breath for it, and her cousin now had to come to see her, if they were to meet at all.

'Have you done anything about the flat?' Alexia asked David.

'I asked Nell to let me know if she hears of anything,' he said lamely.

Someone, thinking Cressy in an advanced condition, gave her a stool. She sat down thankfully.

'We have a cousin who is an estate-agent in Hammersmith,' Alexia said. 'I'll give you his address. He might be some use to you. Have you got a pencil?' She never carried a handbag.

David gave her a pen. He said, 'I'm really rather worried about Mother. I asked her to come with us this morning, but she's not well. She sounded terrible on the phone.'

'I would have thought her awfully strong,' Alexia said. 'All that gardening.'

'Yes, it's not like her. Perhaps she's overdone it – us staying there all that time.'

'Well, I dare say she'll be better in a day or two. Here, I've written on this.' Alexia handed him a beer mat on which she had scribbled her cousin's address. 'I feel sure he might be useful.'

'That's awfully kind,' David said. 'I'll get in touch.' He put the beer mat in his pocket.

'He won't get in touch,' Alexia said later to Toby, while they were having lunch. 'That woman has them in thrall – especially the girl. She pets her, and spoils her, does all her thinking for her, and stuffs her up like a Strasbourg goose.'

'I don't care,' Toby said.

'Cressy fought that battle with her grandfather, but this one she'll never fight. She doesn't even know there's a war.'

CHAPTER FIFTEEN

Midge, some weeks later, was having Sunday tea at the cottage. The threat had seemed to be shadowing her less of late; for nothing had been said. And David was working in the garden, as if he had half-hearted plans for it.

With Cressy on her own, she had sometimes started conversations which could have led to the subject, but never had; and she thought the girl too simple, and too lazy, to dissemble, or to hide anything.

She was alone in the room for a little while. David was still working in the garden, and Cressy had gone to the kitchen to make the tea. Midge looked about her. On a desk – David's old desk from his bedroom at home – was a pile of duplicated sheets. She knew at once from their lay-out that they were from an estate-agent. She got up and went to look at them. An estate-agent in Hammersmith. Glancing round her, and out of the window at David in the garden, she quickly went through them. Agencies from Hampstead and Highgate, too. Trembling, she went back to her chair and sat down. She listened in a confused way to Cressy banging about in the kitchen, and presently David came stamping into the house, kicking off his boots in the hall. He came into the room, looking vaguely about for something to put on his feet, a toe poking out of a hole in his sock.

'That bloody garden,' he said. 'You can't beat it. The weeds grow three feet as soon as I turn my back.'

She smiled with trembling lips.

'Are you all right?' he suddenly asked, staring at her. 'You're as white as a sheet.'

'Of course I'm all right,' she said, in a neat, bright voice.

'Well you don't look it. Is it this back of yours?'

'It is no one else's.' Her tone was flippant.

'Have you seen Dr Baseden yet? You promised me you would.'

'Yes, I've seen him.'

'What did he say?'

'He hasn't a clue. He implied that backs were beyond him. The one thing he can do nothing about. He just gave me something to help me sleep.'

'You don't sleep then?'

She looked at him, said nothing, and looked away.

She had in fact seen Dr Baseden, and had even felt annoyed with him for suggesting no way of curing her, and had resented his questions, which seemed to her to have nothing to do with her physical condition.

'What a pretty cake,' she said brightly, changing the subject as Cressy came in with the tray.

'It's only a Walnut Tree one,' Cressy said, as if one of her own making would have been better.

After tea, Midge suggested a walk round the garden. 'I can't sit still for long,' she explained. 'I get stiff.' She got up with difficulty, and went outside with David.

'You see what I mean?' he asked, looking gloomily at the tangled growth.

She did see, for it would have been too much for *her*, much as she liked gardening, and challenge: but, as usual, she was able to find possibilities, and had all kinds of optimistic suggestions, although she was sympathetic to him about his problems.

'Well, that's that,' he said. 'Let's go in and have a drink. You look tired out.'

'A drink would be lovely.'

Back in the sitting-room she said, 'I've been thinking, David. Cressy. I wonder if you would like me to get some contractors in and get that garden straight once and for all. Then all you'll have to do is keep it tidy. It's such a bore for you to have to spend your precious week-ends slaving away at it. It could be your birthday present from me, David. I can ring up some people I know tomorrow, and then it will all be set for the rest of the summer.'

He frowned. He leaned down and tried to pull his sock over the hole in the toe, and then said, 'It's very generous of you, Mother. And thoughtful. But please don't. It might be such a frightful waste of money. You see . . . I've not said anything before, for nothing's settled . . . but we may not be here much longer. I've thought about it a great deal, and I'm sure I'm right. We've decided to go to live in London, if we can find somewhere. I can't stand much more of living in the country. Nothing seems to go right for us here. And I don't think I could bear another winter. I only bother about the garden, so that it won't look too much of a wilderness when I come to sell.'

Midge settled a cushion in the small of her back.

'I'm sure you're right,' she said. 'I've thought of this myself for a long time. But I didn't want to interfere.'

He stared at her with a look of incredulous relief. Then he said, 'I've only been worried about you. Especially as you're not well.'

'Good heavens, why? I can look after myself.'

'But you'll be lonely.'

'I shall miss you, of course; but I can sometimes come to see you in London. Cressy and I can have lunch together; can't we, darling.'

'We shall still worry.'

Midge looked thoughtful. 'The older I grow, the more I realise,' she said, 'that one never really knows about other people. What one person must have, another doesn't need. And, in a way, I don't need people at all. I've never really troubled to make any friends. One had one's children, but they grow up, and it comes to an end. One knows it's going to happen, and quite right, too, that it should.'

David got up and refilled her glass. 'I must confess you've taken a load off my mind,' he said, smiling.

'And *you'd* take a load off *my* mind if you'd put something on your feet.'

Cressy had been looking nervous during this conversation. 'Does anyone mind if I have the television on?' she asked.

'Well, that's marvellous,' Nell said. 'It's almost too good to be true. Now you'll really have to get moving.' 'Before Midge changes her mind,' she meant. She said, 'You've missed too many chances already.' Why should I care? she wondered.

They were in the city pub at lunchtime.

'We shan't be able to leave until after the baby's born.'

'Why ever not?'

'Cressy doesn't want to. She's going into the nursing-home at Market Harbury. It was all fixed up months ago.'

'Well, she could still go there, couldn't she? It's not all that far.'

'She thinks it is. And so does Mother. And I suppose they know more about it than I do. And, after all, we might as well have the rest of the summer in the country. I don't mind the drive in the light evenings.'

In fact, he didn't. He now had his regular stopping-places, where he would call in for a pint of beer and a piece of pie, arriving home late; and Cressy had hardly ever complained.

Nell yawned. 'I give up,' she said. 'It's not my affair. And now I must go. I've got work to do this afternoon.'

That night, Cressy did complain. She had suddenly, about eight o'clock, felt restless. Sitting for so long before the television had given her cramp, and pins-and-needles in her feet. When David arrived, she was woeful.

'I'm sorry, darling,' he said, taking her into his arms. 'I truly thought you didn't mind. It's such a long, tedious journey without a break, and I ran into someone I know.'

'The same old story,' she said, but she clasped him tightly to her.

'My dear little fatty,' he said, stroking her hair. 'I love you very much. I won't do it again, I promise. As long as you don't cry,' he added hastily. 'And when we get to London, it will be quite different. I'll be home by half past six every evening of the week. Is there anything for supper?'

'Yes, of course.' She released herself from his arms, and looked about vaguely.

'Why no telly?' he asked.

'Oh, it gets on my nerves. I've got a pain here,' she said, pressing her hand to her side. 'It's like toothache in my ribs, and the television only makes it worse.'

'I think you need a change, and I've a good idea. I heard this morning that Jack and I have to go to Normandy for a week – to write up the landing beaches. Why don't you come too?'

'Oh, I couldn't like this,' she said, looking down at her stomach, like a little girl who is asked to a party and hasn't a clean dress.

'Why not?'

'I look so awful, and I shouldn't be comfortable sitting in the car.'

'You could speak your lovely French.'

'Oh, no, no. It's not lovely at all.'

'You used to want to go everywhere and see everything – and I've taken you nowhere and shown you nothing.'

Much of his great enjoyment in her company had been her unspoiled pleasures and enthusiasms.

'When the baby's born you'll never get away,' he said. He followed her into the kitchen, where slowly she began to cut a slice of bread. She switched on the grill.

'I couldn't go,' she said.

'You won't make the effort.'

She stood guard over the piece of toast, turned it over, said nothing.

'I'm not too keen on leaving you here on your own,' he said.

In spite of her standing guard over it, somehow, while she looked away for a moment, the toast was burned. She took it to the sink and began to scrape it.

'I'm sure your mother would let me stay with her,' she said.

'Of course you can stay,' Midge said to her the next day. 'Whenever you like, and for as long as you like. I'll see that you're taken care of.'

They were having coffee at the kitchen table, for Midge had been arranging flowers at the sink when Cressy called. She went on stripping leaves off stems into an old newspaper.

'Do have another biscuit,' she urged Cressy.

'I really shouldn't. Dr Baseden's quite cross with me. He says I'm putting on too much weight.'

'Dr Baseden's an old fool,' Midge said. 'Try one of those ginger ones.'

CHAPTER SIXTEEN

Pet's baby son was just what Harry wanted at the time. The child came most usefully for him, and Pet spent many dumb and tedious hours in the studio with the child in her lap, or at her breast. She was meek in her manner, feeling that she had better be, in her state of complete dependence. She even consented to be sketched sitting sideways on a donkey with the child in her arms, looking as apathetic as any refugee. The baby was placid, and made no fuss, as if he, too, knew his situation.

Everything seemed to work out to the Master's advantage – except the new houses encroaching upon Quayne. They were almost completed. Soon voices would rise from them, television aerials go up on the rooftops, and commuting cars disturb the quiet of Quayne Hill. The lane would be straightened, widened; more trees would be felled and more houses built, his peace destroyed, their community jarred by the outside world. He often thought now of moving away, of finding some real country while there was any left, of beginning again, building a new chapel. He told no one of his plans, not even his wife. They would all receive instructions when the time was ripe. He thought of Suffolk, and decided to make for there on his next walking-tour with Leofric.

Midge took Cressy to see Pet's baby; but stayed by her car in the lane. She spent the time digging up leaf-mould from the woods to enrich her garden. Rose, hearing of it, thought her behaviour very rude.

The baby had lain peacefully in its wooden rocking-cradle.

'We used to sell those in the shop. People keep logs in them,' Cressy said.

'And I suppose put their babies to sleep in the coal scuttle,' Pet said scornfully.

'Did it hurt?' Cressy asked, looking down at the baby.

'Not in the least,' said Pet, stretching out a toe to rock the cradle.

'That's all right then,' Cressy said, feeling she really had not the energy to suffer pain. She wished the time would come, be over. The weather was so warm, and her feet were swollen. She could hardly walk back across the courtyard and down the lane to Midge's car.

The last few days – and the nights – seemed never-ending. She was discontented. Now she wished that she had a cradle like Pet's. It would make a baby seem more of a toy. 'I never thought you would be envious of *her*,' David said reprovingly.

Midge had packed the suitcase for the nursing-home, and it stood ready by the front door, as if to be snatched up in great haste.

'I don't know what I'd do without you,' Cressy said to her. 'If David were at work, and you weren't there, what should I do?'

'Don't worry about what can't happen,' Midge replied.

In the end, it was she who took Cressy to the nursing-home, as she had always, for no reason, supposed it would be. She drove her there one hot afternoon – Cressy, with vague, upsetting pains, sighing and shuffling about beside her, nervously wiping her moist palms on her skirt.

'I think it will rain,' Midge said, looking at the cloudy sky. 'Then we shall all be more comfortable.'

Cressy could not be interested in anyone's comfort but her own.

At the nursing-home everyone seemed casual and unconcerned about her. They implied that, later on, when they found they had nothing better to do, they might attend to her. Midge drove back to the cottage to wait for David.

The baby was born early the next morning – a son.

David, hearing the news, was suddenly overwhelmed with excitement. He had not imagined feeling like this. His dreary worries, his shrinking from responsibility left him. Now he wanted to make known his importance to everyone in the world. He spent hours on the telephone: he could not stop talking.

'My *real* grandchild,' Midge said to Mrs Brindle. 'The others are just little people in photographs.'

'You've never seemed like a grandmother to me,' Mrs Brindle said. 'I doubt if I'll ever see you in that light.'

When, later that day, David went to the nursing-home, he found Cressy looking very neat, with her long hair tied in two bunches by pieces of tape. He put his roses down on the locker beside the bed. (Flowers from Midge had arrived already, and were in hideous vases round the room.) Bending down to kiss Cressy, he thought she smelled very unfamiliar and antiseptic.

'It *did* hurt,' she said accusingly. 'It hurt like hell.'

'It's all over now. But I was so worried I couldn't sleep.'

'I couldn't sleep either. What did you have for supper?'

'Oh . . . I can't remember. Mother got something.'

'I had nothing.'

The baby was asleep in a cot across the room, and he went

over rather self-consciously to look at him. He was veined and downy, like a small animal, David decided, staring down at him but, it was the fact of his *being* that excited him; not what he was at this moment. He stayed politely by the cot for a moment or two, hoping that his worries were not returning to him. Cressy watched him complacently.

'Don't you think "Timothy" is nice?' she asked. 'Midge liked it.'

'Yes. I don't mind.'

'Is she pleased – Midge?'

'You bet she's pleased. And so is your mother.'

'Oh, Mother thinks he has been born in sin. I suppose she pities him.'

'She does nothing of the kind. And your father's delighted, too. This evening, I'm going to celebrate with him at the Three Horseshoes.'

'I wish I could come.'

'We'll have a special little party when you're at home again.'

'Will Midge come to see me?'

'Nothing will keep her away,' David said.

When Midge came, she spent most of the time rearranging the flowers. It was peaceful, Cressy thought sleepily, having her there, just softly moving about the room.

When the baby cried, she stooped over the cot and turned him gently on to his other side.

'I don't think you're allowed to touch him,' Cressy said. But the baby was quiet at once.

At first, the child looked sun-tanned, as if he had just come from the South of France, not Cressy's womb. Then his face took on a yellow tinge, and his eyes were bloodshot. He smelled waxy, when he did not smell of sick. He had screamed all night in the nursery, Cressy was always told when he was brought in at six o'clock. He had disturbed the other babies.

David was worried, and Cressy was usually in tears when he called on his way home from work. The mood of celebration had worn off. Rose came to see the baby, and was unable to hide her anxiety. Only Midge was any comfort to Cressy. She had consoling recollections – of her own first-born with jaundice, of how common it was in infants, and how soon it disappeared.

'And I had everything primrose,' she said. 'His cot draped with it, the pillows, the blankets, and there he lay like a little shrivelled blood orange amongst it all. You really mustn't worry.'

'But if he goes on screaming when I get him home?'

'I'm sure he won't. But if he does, I'll be there to help you.'

Cressy sighed and shut her eyes. She was so tired, she explained. Six o'clock in the morning was terrible, and sometimes a nurse brought the child at half past five. She was made to get out of bed for most of the day, and join the other mothers while they bathed their babies, and to hear again that it was her son who had upset them all at night.

'If only I could stay in bed and have a rest,' she said to Midge.

'I was kept in bed for a fortnight when I had mine,' Midge said. 'And I think that's right. After all, we're not peasants.'

CHAPTER SEVENTEEN

It had been some months since David had called to see his father. The summer had gone by, and autumn was in the air. Even from the outside, the house now had a look of neglect. The windows were dusty, and the brass door-knocker was dull. After a long time, in which David could hear a slow shuffling downstairs and along the passage, Archie opened the door. He was wearing a dressing-gown.

Oh, God, now *he's* ill, David thought angrily.

His father's face seemed to have become very soft and small and blurred and, following him down the passage, David saw the frailty of his corded neck, the deep hollow at the base of his skull. Like a baby's the head seemed to bob about involuntarily.

'I hope you will excuse my dishabille,' Archie said, opening the drawing-room door. 'I was about to have an early night.'

It was not yet seven o'clock.

David made a vague apology; but for what he was not quite sure.

'No, no, my boy!' Archie protested. 'I'm delighted to see you. One does not have many callers.'

He lowered himself into a chair and looked about the room,

as if he had not entered it for a long time. 'And how've you bin keeping?' he asked politely.

'Are you ill, Father?' David asked, fearful of the answer.

'Nothing at all to worry about. A touch of the colley-wobbles, as I believe you young people call it.'

David had never heard the word, and dreaded details.

The room was cold and stuffy. It smelled of dusty carpets, dandruff, sour breath, decay. He longed to fling up the sashed windows.

'Mrs Thing comes less and less,' Archie said, looking calmly at a tarnished silver vase holding fog-coloured pampas grass. 'One's standards are inevitably relaxed a little.'

To David it was always an astonishing thing to find that people are capable of changing, can be a totally different person between one year's beginning and end. For this reason he rejected his father's image of Midge – she was not like that, so could not have been – and was so bewildered by Cressy's trans-formation. He would not have believed father and mother had reversed roles, Archie going sluttishly about the house in his dressing-gown, as he had always described Midge.

'How is my grandson?' Archie asked, with a pleased, coy look up at David.

'He hasn't made a very good beginning, poor Timmy.'

'Ah, yes, Timothy. A good enough name for a small boy; but hardly suitable for an old man. Perhaps you didn't think that far ahead. What's the matter with him?'

'He cries a lot. We have awful nights.' (*I have awful nights* was more to the point, David thought; for Cressy slept heavily.) 'He hasn't put on as much weight as he should. He gets indi-gestion.'

'Ah, the colley-wobbles. You should call in the medico. Mine gave me some tablets. They quieten it down a little.'

Not much, David thought; for the old stomach was chirping

161

and bubbling gassily, and Archie kept banging a fist at his lower ribs, and smothering belches.

'And your lady-wife?' he asked in a fastidious, mocking tone. *Her* name had escaped him, too.

'Well, thank you.'

David got up and walked about the dusty room. 'Mother was burgled some time back,' he said.

'I hope they didn't get off with too much,' Archie said quickly, wondering if David had come from an ulterior motive. 'I'm afraid there's nothing doing in this direction.'

'I don't know what you mean. They made a Godawful mess and stole her diamond ear-rings.'

'My *mater's* diamond ear-rings,' Archie said, remembering. 'Fully insured,' he added. 'Or *were.*'

'They went through all her drawers – just tipped them out on the floor. Something may have disturbed them before they found her other jewellery. She had only been out of the house half an hour. She had just come down to bring Cressy some apple jelly she'd made.'

'I've no doubt it was the servant who made the apple jelly,' Archie said sarcastically. 'I was forever having to tell her about locking doors. Would she listen? She would not. It was just too much trouble to turn the key in the lock, or run the bolt along. I am only astonished it hasn't happened before. You called the police in, I take it?'

'Oh, yes, they came and put powder over everything, looking for fingerprints, but only found Mother's.'

'Ah, they wore gloves, no doubt. Artful customers, these burglars. You never know what little trick they're going to think of next. Well, it was quite an adventure for you all. And I can't see that your mother can complain, for I never saw her wear those ear-rings in her life. Couldn't have done, for that matter, because she refused to have her ears pierced. Between you and me, she preferred flashier baubles. She came to me with nothing else.'

'She was dreadfully upset. And *that* upset all our plans. Cressy and I were thinking of moving to London; but how can we go now, and leave her there so isolated? Well, Cressy says we can't. She's devoted to Midge.'

'Extraordinary,' Archie murmured, and then went on uneasily, 'Moving to London, did you say? Well, it's not easy to find anywhere, or so I hear. Perhaps you are thinking that it is selfish of me to keep a house like this to myself. I don't know if that was in your mind. But at my age I'm afraid that I don't feel up to having a young child about me. Especially if he cries as much as you say.'

The idea behind this appalled David. He imagined them etiolated, suffocated in smelly darkness.

'Don't worry, it won't happen,' he said, as much to reassure himself as his father. That was one terrifying hazard he had not foreseen, so had not had to worry about it.

'I don't know if there is anything left to drink,' Archie said. 'I seldom take anything now, and keep no tally of it.'

'I must go, anyhow.' Making a getaway, he thought of it.

His father at once began to heave himself out of his chair. Yes, it was the smell of sebum, of greasy hair, David realised, going to help him. Strange, because Archie had none, was palely bald.

'I hope you'll be all right. Always let me know if you're not.'

'Don't worry. I am at peace,' Archie said, and the death-bed words alarmed David even more.

The usual shame came over him as he drove away, shame for his negligence, and for his lack of any but the most selfish feelings.

Now I'm going to be late home anyway, he thought, and decided to be later still. He made his way back to Nell's flat to ask her out to dinner. Nell, however, had just washed her hair. She wound a scarf into a turban round her head and, leaving him to pour out a drink, took up some covered dishes and went out to the Chinese restaurant to fetch some sweet and sour pork for their supper.

'He didn't come home at all,' Cressy told Midge. 'He rang up to say that he'd worked too late.'

'Where from?' Midge took off her gloves, smoothed them carefully, as if she were absorbed in the task.

'What do you mean where from?'

'Where was he when he telephoned?'

'Oh, I see. At Jack Ballard's. He had some supper there and stayed the night.'

Well, it was asking for trouble, this marriage, Midge thought. She remembered a saying of her father's – Be careful what you want: you might get it.

'The night seemed so long,' Cressy complained. 'Tim cried and cried.'

By the look of her, so had *she*, Midge thought.

'It's maddening to prepare dinner for someone who never arrives,' she said slyly. She made the remark only for her own satisfaction, and let it go lightly, turning away to pick up the baby, who had begun to cry again. He had been sick – but not recently – and his woolly jacket was stiff and sour-smelling. She put him against her shoulder and patted his back, and a long chain of dribble settled on her collar, and was smeared against her cheek.

Cressy's room was like a stage-set for some depressing play about young-married strife, the very background for bickering and disillusion. Napkins steamed round the fire; the ironing-board was piled high with unironed clothes, and the table with unwashed crockery. There was a feeding-bottle, empty, but with a curdy deposit round its sides.

Daringly, but feeling that she must rescue her grandson, Midge said, 'I think it's easier if one sterilises the bottles at once; and then leave them in cold water until they're wanted.'

Cressy looked blank.

'Otherwise . . . one can't be too careful. The slightest thing can cause a tummy upset.'

'He's got one already.'

'Yes, he's windy; aren't you, my poor darling? He keeps trying to draw his knees up.'

She walked up and down the room – her usual perambulating, but now to soothe Timmy, not herself. She picked her way round between table and ironing-board and pram, and Cressy watched her without hope. But, at last, the baby's eyelids dropped, his wet lips parted, and he slept.

'He's gone off,' Midge said softly. He had become heavier in her arms, as sleeping children do. 'Shall I take him upstairs?'

'He'll only start to cry again. I just put him in his pram. It saves a lot of running up and down stairs.'

'Let's try. He'll sleep better if he's undisturbed.'

She carried him carefully upstairs and laid him in his cot. His eyelids fluttered for a moment, but then he put his thumb in his mouth, curved his fingers round his nose, and slept.

Midge, looking down at him, almost afraid to make a movement, was stirred by anxiety. He looked careworn, not like a baby at all. His eyelids were mauve, and his face shadowy and pale. His scalp was thickly scaly, and he smelled of sicked-up milk.

I could make something of him, she thought, feeling a sense of power strengthening her, and her concern for him strengthening that. If she had ever loved her own young children as much, it was so long ago that she had forgotten.

She crept downstairs, and nodded triumphantly at Cressy, who was shame-facedly trying to clean the feeding-bottle.

'I really only looked in to see if you wanted anything in the village,' Midge said. 'But I could stay for a bit, if you'd like me to give you a hand.'

'Stay for ever,' Cressy said. 'I hate it on my own.'

'It's a special sort of loneliness, being tied to the house with a sick baby. I can remember,' Midge said, taking off her coat. But she could not remember. She was using her imagination.

Briskly, she plugged in the iron, and began to sort out the pile of clothes. David's shirts were so badly washed that she longed to do them again. She was ironing in dirt, she told herself. His life – her son's – had changed, and no mistake.

'I can't believe in silence,' Cressy marvelled. 'It's simply like magic.'

All the same, they spoke in low voices.

'You're run-down and overtired, I think,' Midge said. 'Any time you want a sure night's rest, I'll have Tim. There's David's old cot up in the loft. Rather shabby, but I can paint it. Then it will always be there when wanted. I mean to be useful, you know.'

While she ironed, her mind went from one detail to another, making plans, for days far, far ahead.

CHAPTER EIGHTEEN

After his visit to the hospital, David returned to Nell's flat. Fog, for a week, had made a nightmare of the drive home. He had attempted it the evening before and had arrived very late and out-of-humour, to find Cressy out-of-humour, too.

'If I had known, I could have spent the evening with Midge,' she had complained. 'You don't realise how lonely it is here. If I put the television on it wakes Tim up.'

'So you'd rather take the poor little bugger out in the fog?'

'Midge would have fetched us and brought us back, and he would have been wrapped up warm, and in his carry cot.'

He knew that it would have been that way round: for Midge liked to have about her what she had created.

'You're so irresponsible it's unbelievable.'

He had described it all to Nell. 'I told her I'd save myself the trouble today. "You can go and spend the night with Mother," I said. "You can move in, lock, stock and barrel, for all I bloody care." I didn't mean that last, of course. One loses one's temper. The thing is she simply can't manage the baby, and is afraid to be left alone with it.'

'And Midge can manage it?'

'Oh, yes, she can manage it all right. She's made a dear little nursery for him, and sometimes she takes him off for the night, so that Cressy can have a good sleep. But Cressy's always had a good sleep. It's not Cressy who gets up in the night, and traipses up and down with the poor little fellow.'

'How was your father?' Nell asked, sprawled on the divan, nursing her little dog. She was tired of the subject of Cressy – that moronic child, as she thought of her. David had certainly married in haste to repent at leisure. He took his time about it, and hers too.

'Oh, and my father,' David said tiredly, oppressed by all his troubles. 'It looks to me as if he's going out fast. He just lies there taking little sips of air, like a stranded fish. It's horrible to see. And then this awful look comes on his face, and you know he knows he's going to have to cough and is afraid to. One doesn't know how to help or what to say. He hates the whole set-up there. The nurses are so awfully matey, and call him "poppet". My father! Poppet! And they tidy him up, just as if he were a baby. Of course, he worries about the money, though I can't see that he need. "It's all coming out of capital – just to die in private," he says. You know what old people are like about touching capital. You'd think they wouldn't care.'

'Shall we have Chinese again?' Nell asked, tired of all David's subjects.

'Or go round the corner for Italian?' he suggested.

'Yes, let's go round the corner and have Italian,' Nell agreed. 'I am bored of Chinese.' She always said that – 'I am bored of.' A childish expression she had never corrected.

In the street, the fog drifted. Passers-by came suddenly out of it, with the brief sound of footsteps, a snatch of conversation, and were immediately gone. Nell held her fur collar across her mouth, and plodded on grimly.

The Italian restaurant was nothing special. It had the usual plastic vine-leaves climbing up imitation bamboo, a blown-up photograph of the Bay of Naples as a mural, strings of onions, chianti-bottle lamp-holders, and the familiar menu, with melon and so-called Parma ham, and escallopes of veal, and cassata.

David began to relax, putting away from him thoughts of Cressy, the baby, his visit to the hospital. A pleasant bachelor feeling came over him. He poured out more wine and ordered another bottle. His ham – he ought to have known from experience – was mostly stringy fat. If he would not fill himself with canneloni, then Nell should not either, he thought; but watched with pleasure her pleasure as she did so. She wiped the sauce from her plate with a piece of bread, and when that was done, looked up and smiled at him, as if ready now for conversation.

'It's very good of you to listen to all my troubles,' he said.

'Oh, don't mention it.'

'This is like the old days. Do you remember that Spanish one we used to go to?'

'Yes, we've fairly eaten our way round London. At least this doesn't have dressed-up waiters. I'm so bored of their boaters, and butcher's aprons, and gondoliers' hats.'

'And these stinking fishermen's jerseys at the English Fish Parlour. They smell worse than the stale fish. Where do you go nowadays?'

'Mostly nowhere. Since you jilted me I stay at home with my little dog.'

He laughed, for he was sure that he was meant to. 'You always manage to put me in a good humour,' he said.

She sipped her wine, not replying.

'Would you like some brandy?' he asked, when their coffee was brought.

'Oh, yes, please. I'll have the lot if I may,' she said.

'And then I suppose I must get on my way. It will take some time in this fog to get across to Jack's.'

'It probably will,' she said calmly.

'And it's always worse down by the river.'

'Invariably,' she agreed, tipping her glass to get the last drop. She had wrapped some dried-up veal in a paper napkin for her dog, and she put it in her handbag and looked across at him, ready to go home. She was alert, as if expecting him to say something else.

'It might go on for days,' he said, meaning the fog. But tonight, at least, he would go to Chelsea, he decided, rather proud of his resolution.

Down by the river, the fog was much worse. There were hardly any cars, and no footsteps. Jack Ballard was going to bed, when David came back, but he had left the door-key under a shoe-scraper. He was now a fairly fashionable photographer, and could afford his own little house, with a glossy magnolia outside, and a beautiful fanlight, and an outlook of other pretty houses across the road. Tonight nothing of these could be seen, only blurred lights from them suspended in the thick air.

David had a divan in a spare room full of old photography equipment.

They drank some whisky together before turning in. The fog wrapped the house in silence. It had hung up Jack's work for days, and the Street Markets series was interrupted.

'What haven't we *done?*' he asked gloomily, looking ahead.

'The subjects are endless,' David said. 'Name anything: we'll take a look at it.'

'It seems a long time since we came up with anything really clever. The Harry Bretton one was good, you know.'

'Well . . . let me think. Oh, I had an idea the other day. What about the religions of London – get some nice shots of old Salvation Army souls, Greek Orthodox wedding, Jewish circumcision, Irish wake . . .'

'Too many of them.'

'Do another series.'

'People would get tired of it long before the end.'

'What about pavement artists, then?' The ideas came at random, for it was random journalism.

'I should guess there wouldn't be enough of *them*.'

'It's an odd taste, isn't it? Nothing for people to get their teeth into – like eating a jam-puff, gone and forgotten in two shakes. And what the subject is hardly seems to matter – you can hit on anything, and walk round it a couple of times, and ask a few questions, and blow it up and dispose of it.'

'And photograph it in green-greens and blue-blues,' Jack said, of his own part.

'They love that. You make the countryside look quite inviting,' said David, having no love for it.

'Must be a bit laconic occasionally, a bit quirky.'

'Do you remember this sort of journalism when we were young?'

'Perhaps we invented it.'

'You know damn well we didn't.'

'Anyhow, we're stuck with it, and lucky to be so. I think I'll turn in. Not working wears me out. Did you get on much today?'

'I interviewed some chaps in Berwick Street. Nothing wonderfully funny.'

No questions were ever asked about how either had spent the evening – neither where, nor with whom.

David, in his rather cold and very cluttered room, lay awake for a long time, thinking about Cressy and Timmy, his two little children. He tried to feel virtuous that he was lying where he was, and was aggrieved that he could only feel exactly the opposite.

CHAPTER NINETEEN

I shall miss you very much,' Cressy said sadly to her cousin, Pet. 'I can't believe that you are all going away.' Yet she had tried to imagine it, and had succeeded.

They were pushing Pet's baby in his pram round the court-yard at Quayne. Midge had been contented to have Timmy to herself for the afternoon. She would let him lie on the rug before the carefully-guarded fire, and her eyes would rarely leave him. Having him under her roof so much, had made a different child of him. Her authority had given him a sense of security. Only Cressy's timid and uncertain handling made him cry. Once, in an excess of nervousness, she had let him roll from her lap, and Midge had bounded across the room like a lioness, and snatched him up. Her ferocity had alarmed Cressy even more, and she had watched her pacing up and down with the sobbing child in her arms, making soothing noises, laying her cheek against his wet one, kissing him again and again. Every kiss was a reproof to Cressy who, quite ignored, had sat trembling in her chair, her own tears falling into the napkin spread across her knees. For the reason that she could not bear to think of the scene, she had not described it to Pet, to whom she nowadays confided a great deal.

There was no one else about in the courtyard, but they could hear voices from the studio. Their grandfather was there, talking to two young men, of ancient Roman Catholic families and vague artistic leanings, who had been sent to stay at Quayne for a week or two, until something else for them to do had been discovered.

'We might have married *them*,' Cressy said.

'Oh, they are far too grand for us.'

As they went along the mossy brick path under the studio wall, they could hear the Master booming away inside. He had got into a rhythm which seemed to make him reluctant to finish his lengthy sentences. 'The question of what Turner is a-bout,' they heard, going by as quickly as they could, 'is really the question of what painting is a-bout, what art is a-bout; in fact, what life itself, and death itself, is certainly a-bout.'

Pet and Cressy looked at one another, with pursed lips, as if to stop an explosion of laughter. 'It doesn't mean *a* thing,' Pet whispered. 'He hasn't a clue what he is talking a-bout.'

'Does he still make a lot of money?' Cressy asked, when they had gone out of hearing.

'The Lord provides. There's a big job at the moment for a great new church – designing a tapestry and mosaics. I am in them,' Pet added, without pride. She peered into the battered old pram and rearranged the baby against his pillow.

'Suffolk is so far away,' Cressy complained. 'I might never see you again.'

'Couldn't I sometimes come to stay with you? I should love to stay in someone else's house.'

'Well, I suppose you could,' Cressy said doubtfully.

In the kitchen-garden they met Mo, who was cutting some

cabbages, and keeping an eye on the studio door, hoping to intercept the young men when they came out of it. The cabbages were curled and purple and full of raindrops, and their leaves creaked stiffly as she held them in her arms. She was not pleased to see her cousins, for she had hung out her errand as long as she could, and there was no sign of the young men. She did not know that one of them was watching from a window as she crossed the courtyard. He was standing with folded arms, trying to convey frowning attention, looking occasionally sideways down at the ground, not listening to a word about Turner. The other young man presently dared to ask a question about Picasso. It was their only hope of release, and very soon they were allowed to go off across the courtyard towards the house, where bread, they could smell, was being baked on a large scale.

Harry, left alone, was too ruffled to get on with his work. Over the years, he had come to hate Picasso, with a deep, uneasy hatred. He had always detested his work, but now he also detested the creator of it. He was envious of him for remaining, as he himself had not, a controversial figure. To have once been a controversial figure was something to look back on, and to know that he no longer was – or only to the elderly – humiliated him. Once he had scandalised; but to see religious characters in modern clothes and surrounded by everyday odds and ends no longer scandalised anyone. In the good old days, a maniac had jabbed one of his paintings with a pen-knife, and others, more conventional, had jabbed at him in letters to *The Times*: now he was mildly praised by the very generation he had wasped, and ignored by the young.

In his character he had a need to admire other men, and Turner he admired. He had Leofric Welland's book about him in his hands, had been reading passages from it to the young men. Now, he turned the pages slowly, but saw nothing. He put the book down and stood by the window in a dream. He could find it in his heart to worship the man, and doing so enlarged himself. Turner was the greatest English painter, and was safely dead, did not encroach or suggest comparisons. But at the end, he had petered out, not grown and gone ahead like Picasso – grown and gone ahead *monstrously*, Harry considered; in old age he had shown recklessness and a complete lack of humility. It was annoying how his name, once mentioned, could not be put out of Harry's mind. He tried to think, instead, of his own future – of the move into Suffolk and a new life there. They had come, over the years, to lie in a rut, in the sheltered vapours of Quayne; but soon there would be new homes to create, a new generation to influence, new chapters for Leofric's biography; and perhaps, too – who could tell? – his great retrospective exhibition at the Tate.

Cressy, he thought, seeing her from the window, would miss this great spiritual and physical upheaval. In her ignorance of the world and refusal to be taught, her childish rebelliousness, she had simply got out of one rut and into another.

He crossed the studio to his unfinished painting of 'The Raising of Lazarus', and willed the sense of his own greatness to return to him, was practically sure that it had returned to him; and he pointed out to himself, as he might have done to a ring of admiring students, the organisation of the whole, the slanting, fore-shortened figures, and the richness of all the day-to-day textures that he loved so much – herring-boned tweeds and lumpy knitting-stitches, and basket-work and braided hair. Lazarus was in striped pyjamas, for he particularly liked painting striped pyjamas. He tried to concentrate on the picture, on his intentions for it as a whole, and for the as yet unpainted areas; but other, extraneous thoughts came into his mind instead – the words 'Sir Harry Bretton', for instance. That he was *not* – and it would have sounded so well – was a grievance of long-standing. There was also the recurring discomfort of undue homage paid to Francis Bacon – a gathering menace. And the new annoyance of those two young men, with their lack of enthusiasm for his works.

He turned away from the easel, slung his shepherd's cloak over his shoulders, and went out and locked the studio door – the only door which ever was locked at Quayne. The courtyard was empty. Cressy and Pet had gone inside.

He was glad to find Rachel alone in their sitting-room. She knew at once that he was out-of-humour, but she went on with her sewing, and waited as calmly as she could. He came to the fire and held out his hands to warm them. Between stitches, she gave little glances at the hands, as if they might offer a hint of his mood, which his face would have done more directly if she had dared to look at it. He turned the hands over and over as if he were lathering them. They were so familiar to her – square, short-fingered, rather grubby. They told her nothing.

'Rachel,' he said at last, looking down at her bent head, 'where are my old letters to you? I feel like sitting here by the fire and reading them to you.'

She was prompt with her look of pleased anticipation, and put aside her sewing and got up at once.

'You'll be all right,' Pet had said comfortingly to Cressy, as they went towards Rose's cottage for tea. There was a slight stress on her first word. 'You've got the baby, and a husband, and a mother-in-law. Two more people than I have. I shall never have *those* two.'

'Midge seems to lose patience with me nowadays, and David hardly ever comes home during the week,' Cressy said in a piteous tone. It was as if she had lost confidence. She had acquired it, and lost it. 'But don't tell Mother about that,' she added.

'Mrs Brindle, I'm afraid, already has.'

'I suppose she would have,' Cressy said sadly, disappointed in her old ally. 'And what will *she* do when you've gone?'

'Mrs Brindle is always in demand. She might even be persuaded to remain.'

Quayne was to become a private school for problem children, and Cressy could easily imagine that Mrs Brindle would find there an alluring opportunity: and her being there would be a great enrichment to the village.

Pet lifted her good little baby from the pram and they went indoors. Father Daughtry and Joe were sitting by the fire, and Rose came in from the kitchen, carrying the teapot. 'And where is Timmy?' she asked, looking at the other child.

'I left him with Midge. I hate pushing the pram up the hill.'

'I should have liked to have seen my grandson,' Rose said stiffly.

The room looked barer than ever, for Joe had already packed his books, as if he had given up all thought at present of getting his own book out of them.

'Two miles and a half to the nearest pub,' he was saying. 'What sort of a place is that going to be?'

'I've known it worse in Connemara,' said Father Daughtry, as if this were a reason for their cheering up.

They sat round the table and, as Rose poured out the tea, she asked, 'What time will David get home this evening?' She was obliged to look at what she was doing, and not at Cressy.

Cressy put on a candid, but casual expression and said lightly, 'Not at all tonight. Not until Friday. He's doing a thing on London riverside pubs.'

'An interesting subject,' Father Daughtry said, feeling that he could warm to it, wishing that he could have joined in its exploration. 'I can well remember The Prospect of Whitby before it became the rage. There was another at Hammersmith I was fond of. And The City Barge. The dear old City Barge.' He was sure that he could have written the article himself, and from memory. 'To lush at Freeman's Quay. Let's have the derivation, now, Joe.'

Rose, ignoring him, sat – having passed the tea-cups – with her hands clasped in her lap. She wore a look of anxiety, which was so usual with her, however, that nobody but Cressy noticed it.

'It must be lonely for you,' she said, in a disapproving, not commiserating voice. She felt that the marriage, which was not really a marriage, was doomed; and Cressy, reading her thoughts, said cheerfully, 'Lots of husbands are away during the week.'

Pet, for her own sake, changed the subject. 'I wonder what it will be like in Suffolk,' she said, for she had not seen her new home. Rose, who had, described it as remote, but open country, very flat. 'You would not have to push the pram up any hill *there*,' she said to Cressy. 'Or *not* push it up,' she added confusedly.

Midge had spent a peaceful afternoon with Timmy. She had taken him for a little outing in the pram, and he had slept. Now she was playing with him on a rug before the fire, holding up a spoon for him to grasp, watching him, entranced. When he put out his left hand, she made him try again with his right hand. She had a suspicion that he was naturally left-handed, and determined to put this right from the beginning. Soon he became fretful, turning his head impatiently, ignoring the spoon, and hooking his hands and fingers in distracted movements, scuffling his legs on the rug like a rabbit. His face darkened, and he began to cry. It was not time for his bottle so she picked him up and walked round the room, showing him things to appease him – flowers, and photographs, his face in a mirror – and talked to him brightly and soothingly. She took up a fan from a table and fanned him and for a second or two he stared in amazement, his eyelids fluttering; then he became petulant again. She laid down the fan and resumed her pacing. She stopped before the Wedgwood wedding group, and lifted him close to it, telling him a story about it, and he stopped crying, and took in a long breath, like an out-going sigh. 'Pretty,' she cooed to him. 'So pretty.' Suddenly, he put out an uncertain hand, lurched forward, and knocked the ornament from the shelf. 'Oh, God!' she cried in a different voice, and he began to scream. 'No, no!' she said softly against his cheek. 'Not to worry, my darling. It doesn't matter. It doesn't matter a little, tiny bit.' She moved away from the scene of the disaster; but nothing would console him now. She gave up trying, and went to warm his bottle.

When Cressy came home, he had been fed and Midge was sitting with him on her lap, gently rubbing his back.

'Yes, I know, darling. I'm more sorry than I can ever express,' she said, as Cressy stopped short, looking at the fragments of pottery on the floor. 'I lifted Timmy up to see it, too near to the shelf, and he suddenly shot out his arm and knocked it down. Oh, it was stupid of me, and I am so grieved that it's gone. I loved it so much. I hope you will be able to forgive me.'

'Well, it was yours, not mine,' Cressy said, bending down to pick up the pieces. It doesn't matter, she thought. Those days when it would have mattered seemed to have gone.

'No, don't! I'll do that. I was just going to,' Midge said. 'As soon as I'd finished with Timmy. You take him, dear, and get up his wind. There! You want to go to your Mummy, don't you, my darling boy? I'll get a brush and dust-pan.'

She handed over the baby and went out to the kitchen. When she came back, he was crying again.

'That's the first tear there's been from him all afternoon,' she said.

Then I'm not necessary to anyone, Cressy thought.

CHAPTER TWENTY

Archie died.

'Well, you certainly did your duty by him,' Midge told David. 'And it was hardly called for under the circs.'

He felt sad and relieved, and the sadness derived from the relief. He had described the quiet death to her as gently as he could, trying to be careful of her sensibilities: and she had thought that no one can misunderstand a mother so completely as her own children. Usually this had suited her very well, and did so now. When her feelings were on the surface, David looked for something deeper; but her deepest thoughts he never guessed. Archie's death meant nothing to her. She hardly remembered him. Once, she might have been glad to have a dead husband, rather than one who had deserted her; but she no longer cared.

David and his brother Geoffrey went to the funeral. The church was almost empty. Some men, doing repair work inside, went and stood outside in the graveyard and smoked, while the service was going on. David could hear their leisurely voices through an open window.

Afterwards, in the dark, neglected house, the solicitor went through the will. The house itself was left to David, as an extra bequest, and in 'recognition of his constant devotion'. He felt ashamed and put-out before his brother, who nodded and murmured magnanimously at the news. David wondered if his father had pictured him living there one day, with Cressy and the baby, in London at last, and away from Midge in Archie's home, but without Archie there to be bothered by the baby's crying.

The baby, however, was over his crying ways. Midge told herself that she would make something of him in time.

'He's a credit to you,' Mrs Brindle said, and Midge saw nothing wrong with her words. 'He never takes his eyes off of you. Just look at that lovely smile.'

It was the morning that Midge was minding him, while Cressy went to Quayne to say good-bye. He was in his pram, just outside the drawing-room window, and both women kept taking peeps at him. He lay awake staring up at moving leaves, petals floating in the air. Sometimes, he would catch a glimpse of a face, a movement at the window and smile.

'It's real spring-cleaning weather,' Mrs Brindle said. 'The sun shows up everything.' She flicked her duster at a swaying strand of cobweb. 'I'll have to get down to it, I can see that.'

Midge hardly listened, putting on her coat, her gloves, getting ready to set off with Timmy in the pram.

'I wonder what on earth she'd do without you,' Mrs Brindle said, meaning Cressy.

Midge smiled complacently. 'I sometimes wonder, too,' she admitted. 'But I said when he was born that I meant to be useful.'

'I only hope it will keep fine while you're out. It's very on and off, the weather.'

The sun went in for a minute, and dark clouds banked up behind the cherry blossom.

'I shan't go far,' Midge said; but she was determined to go, rain or not, for she loved pushing the pram about the village and, even, because of Timmy, had struck up slight friendships there.

'Well, I'll get on,' Mrs Brindle said, in a wistful voice, as if she were not paid to do so.

Feeling marvellously in charge and exhilarated, Midge pushed the pram down the drive and out into the lane, and the sun came out again, and there was nothing wrong in her world.

At Quayne, footsteps rang on the bare floorboards, and voices echoed in empty rooms. Cressy felt in the way, as removal-men pushed by her with crates of books and china, and all the familiar furniture she had known for ever, the decent, solid oak and elm; the farmhouse chairs and the Welsh dresser, the kitchen table, ribbed from many years of scrubbing. Rose was harassed, Joe melancholy. He felt like a piece of furniture himself, and was sad to be leaving his daughter, or rather, being taken away from her.

'We'll have that smart dinner in a restaurant,' he promised her. 'You'll see, I'll take you yet. We'll meet up in London, and you'll be no end surprised to find how I know my way about there.'

'Please, Joe!' Rose said. 'They want to load that box you're sitting on.'

Harry was in the studio, giving out sharp commands. The men staggered out with 'The Raising of Lazarus', hardly able to keep straight faces.

The old farm wagon had soon after dawn gone grinding slowly down Quayne Hill, with Yves's potter's wheel, and lawn-mowers and garden tools, sawn logs, sacks of old potatoes and two goats. Others had left later, by train, and Cressy had missed saying good-bye to her cousins. Now only Father Daughtry,

Harry and Rachel, Rose and Joe were left to squeeze into the old Rolls-Royce.

Father Daughtry, wearing his dark, shabby rain-coat, paced about in the courtyard, wiping a tear or two from his face, feeling muzzy from last night's farewell-party in the Three Horseshoes. Now he would have to make a new set of cronies, and he scarcely felt up to it at his age. He was in the way, too, he thought. He had so few possessions that he had nothing to do.

When the removal vans had driven off, those who were left gathered in the empty chapel, and Father Daughtry was obliged to say a few prayers – for those who were to come to Quayne, as well as for those who were setting out from it – and thanksgivings for what had been. Cressy, standing back by the door, felt that she was at a funeral: there was the same alloy of sadness and hope and gratitude in the service.

She was unhappily aware that it was nearly time for her farewell to her mother. She felt an uneasy dread, and shame, and knew that she must suffer the terrible emotion of embarrassment. There had always been – or as far back as she could remember – awkwardness between them. Perhaps a better daughter would have made a better mother of Rose, she thought – a submissive daughter of the kind Rose was herself, of the kind she could have understood, and had, perhaps, expected.

I said terrible things to her when I was living here, Cressy recalled, and quickly tried not to recall. The relationship had been sullied by words – her own words – which could never be taken back, and would not, in the nature of words, be forgotten, even if forgiven.

She went timidly out of the chapel before the others and stood waiting in the courtyard, hoping she would not cry. After they had gone, she had the long walk home to face, with her depressed feelings to keep her company.

There was no room for her in the Rolls-Royce. Rachel

brought out baskets of food, and packed them in the car. Then she put her rough hand under Cressy's chin and kissed her. When her parents kissed her, Cressy threw her arms round them and held them tightly for a moment. As far as her mother was concerned, she knew it was too late. She had forced herself to be demonstrative, and it could not do any good. Joe climbed into the high driving-seat, and Harry, before he got in beside him, laid his hand on Cressy's head, as if he were blessing her, but was doubtful of the outcome. She stood crying and waving as they drove away.

Now she was the only one left at Quayne, although she could no longer think of it by that name; for Quayne itself was on the move. To the real country, while it was still there. And when that was real no longer, what then, she wondered. Perhaps it would see Harry out, and then they would all drift apart, and live on God knew what. They had set out, like very proud and scornful refugees, leaving the vulgar threat of modern life, its contagions and encroachments.

She began to walk slowly down the hill, past the Regency-type villas, and the great clearing made about them in the woods. It began to rain, and she felt very dismal, and hoped against hope that Midge would invite her to stay the night.

Midge, too, was caught in the rain. It drummed down on the pram hood and cover, and she went as quickly as she could up the hill towards home, with her head bent and the rain on her face. There was nothing for tea, she thought. She had not bothered to go to the Walnut Tree, and would not get extra wet just to buy cakes for Cressy.

A rainbow Cressy noticed, running to catch up with her. It was just like one of Father Daughtry's corny old sayings, and he was probably remarking on it now, as they drove on towards the promised land.

'Oh, I feel very strange,' she said breathlessly, as she came up with Midge. Midge had heard her, turned briefly to see her coming; but had battled on at the same pace. 'It was like going to a funeral,' Cressy explained. Feeling that she should, she attempted to take over the pram; but Midge went on pushing determinedly. 'They got off all right, then?' she asked, without interest.

'I feel like an orphan,' Cressy said dramatically, but Midge did not reply.

Rain cascaded off the brilliantly green branches, and by the time they reached home they were both very uncomfortable.

They went in through the back door, and Mrs Brindle was there to greet them, with a look of incredulity on her face, and a pair of diamond ear-rings in her outstretched hand.

'In a jar of rice!' she shouted. 'A jar of rice, of all things. I thought I'd taken leave of my senses.'

Midge untied her rain-hood, and shook it carefully over the doormat.

'A jar of rice?' she repeated, after a pause.

'I just couldn't believe my eyes. I was turning out the larder and washing all the jars. I emptied the rice out into a bowl, and there they were. Well, as I say, I simply couldn't believe my eyes.'

'What a most extraordinary thing,' Midge said, beginning to take off her wet coat. 'I'll just see to the baby, and then you must tell us all about it.'

CHAPTER TWENTY-ONE

'I suppose,' Midge said to Cressy, later that day, 'I suppose they were interrupted, and hid them there and meant to come back for them another time. It was rather a clever place, really. And to think I've lived here in blissful ignorance, not knowing what they meant to do. Quite honestly, it makes me more nervous than ever.'

'Who could have interrupted them?' Cressy asked. 'They were gone when you got back.'

'Well, anything might have – anything, anybody.' But tradesmen all called in the morning, and she had no friends. 'The telephone even,' she suggested. But no one ever rang up. 'People are always coming here to collect for something – poppies and life-boats and the cruelty to children.'

'Well, as long as you've got them back again. They must be awfully valuable.'

'Yes, I doted on them.'

'What about the insurance?'

'Yes, of course, that. *They* must be told. One feels rather foolish.'

They were having tea, and Cressy could not help thinking of

the days when éclairs were urged upon her. Midge was trying to feed Timmy with some sieved prunes. He put his arm out sternly, warding off another spoonful. She kept scooping it from his chin and pushing it back between his lips. What he had in his mouth he allowed to stay there for a little, and then, frowning, bent his head and dribbled it on to the tray of his high chair.

The invitation to stay the night was not, as was usual, forthcoming. Midge seemed absent-minded, almost as if, for once, she wished to be alone.

'I suppose I had better start thinking about going home,' Cressy said, leaning back in her chair. She wondered if Midge had heard her – she seemed so occupied with Timmy, and made no reply. 'Damn, it's beginning to rain again.' A few threads of rain slanted across the window and, glancing out at them, Cressy suddenly said, 'Good heavens, here's David.'

His car had turned into the drive, and she watched him getting out of it. 'I haven't a thing for supper,' she said.

'I'm afraid I can't ask you to stay here,' Midge said. 'I was just going to have an egg myself. He shouldn't come and go without warning. I should be awfully annoyed if I were you.'

'I guessed I'd find you here,' David said, when Cressy opened the door to him. Rather unexpectedly, for these days, he took her in his arms and kissed her.

She was not in the least annoyed with him, and said, 'How nice and early you are. I only wish I had some food in the house.'

'Hasn't it been one of the nicest evenings?' David asked her, as they drove along the wet motor-way.

Midge had kept Timmy for the night, and David and Cressy had gone out to a pub, and eaten infra-red-ray steaks, as Cressy called them, in a bar full of brass and copper and humorous notices, such as 'Do not leave the bar when it is still in motion' and 'God bless our mortgaged house', done in poker-work. Over a low doorway were the words 'Duck or Grouse', and the lavatories were called 'Lasses' and 'Lads'.

'I wish you could always come home early,' Cressy said.

'Well, of course, I can't. But I made a special effort today, because I thought you'd be a bit down, saying good-bye to your parents.' This was a sudden inspiration, and his words went down very well.

It was really a growing wariness that had made him leave London early that afternoon; for Nell had telephoned him from one of her outside jobs to ask him to pick up some smoked salmon on his way back to her flat – simply assuming that he was going there. The reasonableness of the assumption had alarmed him. He knew that she had every right to expect him, for they had fallen into such a routine that his weekdays had become more like a married life than his weekends.

'It has been quite a day,' said Cressy. 'What with all that sadness at Quayne, and Mrs Brindle finding the ear-rings.'

'*That* has finally decided me,' David said. 'If it hadn't been for the so-called break-in, we'd have been living in London by now.' And all the involvement with Nell would never have begun, he thought. As far as that was concerned, he knew that he was tired of being mothered and patronised and ticked off for his little failings, like unpunctuality and irritability. Even in bed, Nell condescended to him, was too gracious for words, like a very grand hostess with a guest of not much consequence.

'Well, thank God, it's not too late,' he told Cressy, thinking of London, and of a new and different life there with her, which would make a continuation of the Nell affair impossible.

When his father's house was sold, he would have that

much more money to further his plans. They might even be able to afford a little house in Chelsea, like Jack Ballard's, or somewhere a bit out, but equally pleasant and fashionable, such as Chiswick or Blackheath. Apart from his first astonished condemnation, he could not bring himself to say much to Cressy about his mother, whom he saw in such a new light – perhaps Archie's light – that he did not yet recognise her.

'I have never been in one of those motor-way cafés,' Cressy said. 'And I'm still a bit hungry, I'm afraid. There's one in half a mile. May we?'

'Of course we may, if you want. But I don't think you'll find it very nice.'

In half a mile they turned in towards the bright lights, which were blurred in the rain, and ran from the car towards the building. He winced, hearing the pounding of the juke-box, but felt quite cheerful all the same, seeing her eager look as they queued at the self-service counter. Fluorescent light fell on the perspex-enclosed food on cardboard plates.

She really fits in with her generation, he thought – in spite of Quayne and all that that entailed. She was quite content to stand in line, obediently holding her plastic tray.

He looked with horror at a caseful of curled-up fish in batter, at bright yellow cakes covered with shaggy coconut.

In front of them were black-coated, very much studded, motor-bike boys, all wet, but docile. Cressy seemed to go mad in her enthusiasm, helping herself to a pork pie, a cheese roll, little packets of Ryvita and butter, a jelly with a very white whirl of cream on top, and a cardboard beaker of coffee. David marvelled at her appetite. He took a sausage-roll and coffee, and they found a table which had just been wiped down, its sauce bottles re-grouped, and its ash-tray emptied.

The noise was deafening.

'*Our* place,' Cressy said, smiling across the table at him. 'Our little secret hide-out.'

He smiled back at her, between sips of his scalding-hot but tasteless coffee.

'I'm so really happy,' she said. 'And this morning, I didn't feel I would be for a long time.'

'And I feel, too, that it's all going to be different for us from now on.'

'Yes, it will be very exciting.'

She suddenly thought, in a fluster of fear, of having Timmy to look after on her own, her sole responsibility; but, as quickly, she brushed the idea aside. She told herself that the worst with him was over, that she would manage, be happy and confident with him, as she felt, this evening, she was with David.

'We can't be disturbed tonight,' she said, thinking complacently of their being in bed. It would be the final treat of the evening. Meanwhile, she was in this exciting and extraordinary place, with its life of its own; and enjoying herself.

'I'll take you to really nice restaurants in London,' David promised. 'I've never had a chance to show you my favourite places.'

All these dinners in London, she thought – her father coming into her mind fleetingly. Kind, kind, poor father. She unwrapped her butter carefully. 'Look at this dear little plastic knife,' she said.

'Everything disposable – except this sausage-roll by me,' David replied.

In the night, Timmy cried, and Midge heard him at once. She went to his room and lifted him from his cot and carried him, wrapped in a blanket, back to her own bed.

Lying beside her, he soon dropped off to sleep again. She did

191

not want to sleep herself; simply liked having him there with her. Her heart had grown large with love.

Sometimes he stirred and sighed, and she could hear him peacefully sucking his thumb. Blissfully content, in spite of the dangers of the day, at last she fell asleep herself.

MRS PALFREY AT THE CLAREMONT

Elizabeth Taylor

Introduced by Paul Bailey

'An author of great subtlety, great compassion and great depth'
Sarah Waters

On a rainy Sunday afternoon in January, Mrs Palfrey, recently
widowed, arrives at the Claremont Hotel where she will spend
her remaining days. Her fellow residents are a mixed bunch –
magnificently flawed and eccentric – living off crumbs of
affection and an obsessive interest in the relentless round of
hotel meals. Together, upper lips stiffened, they fight off their
twin enemies: boredom and the Grim Reaper. And then one
day, Mrs Palfrey encounters the handsome young writer Ludo,
and learns that even the old can fall in love . . .

'A wonderful novelist' Jilly Cooper

'The unsung heroine of British twentieth-century fiction'
Rebecca Abrams, *New Statesman*

'Elizabeth Taylor had the keenest eye and ear for the pain
lurking behind a genteel demeanour' Paul Bailey

A VIEW OF THE HARBOUR

Elizabeth Taylor

Introduced by Sarah Waters

'Elizabeth Taylor is finally being recognised as an important British author: an author of great subtlety, great compassion and great depth. I have found huge pleasure in returning to Taylor's novels many times over' Sarah Waters

In the faded coastal village of Newby, everyone looks out for – and in on – each other. So, although keeping up appearances is second nature, nothing goes unnoticed for very long. Beautiful divorcée Tory is secretly involved with her neighbour Robert, while his wife, consumed by the worlds she creates in her novels, is oblivious to the relationship developing next door. Their daughter Prudence, however, is appalled by the treachery she observes. Meanwhile Mrs Bracey, an invalid whose grasp on life is slipping, forever peers from her window, gossiping with everybody who passes by.

'Her stories remain with one, indelibly, as though they had been some turning point in one's experience' Elizabeth Bowen

'A wonderful novelist' Jilly Cooper

You can order other Virago titles through our website: *www.virago.co.uk*
or by using the order form below

☐	At Mrs Lippincote's	Elizabeth Taylor	£7.99
☐	A View of the Harbour	Elizabeth Taylor	£8.99
☐	Angel	Elizabeth Taylor	£8.99
☐	In a Summer Season	Elizabeth Taylor	£7.99
☐	Mrs Palfrey at the Claremont	Elizabeth Taylor	£8.99
☐	The Soul of Kindness	Elizabeth Taylor	£8.99
☐	A Game of Hide and Seek	Elizabeth Taylor	£7.99
☐	Palladian	Elizabeth Taylor	£7.99
☐	Blaming	Elizabeth Taylor	£8.99

The prices shown above are correct at time of going to press. However, the publishers reserve the right to increase prices on covers from those previously advertised, without further notice.

Please allow for postage and packing: **Free UK delivery.**
Europe: add 25% of retail price; Rest of World: 45% of retail price.

To order any of the above or any other Virago titles, please call our credit card orderline or fill in this coupon and send/fax it to:

Virago, PO Box 121, Kettering, Northants NN14 4ZQ
Fax: 01832 733076   Tel: 01832 737526
Email: aspenhouse@FSBDial.co.uk

☐ I enclose a UK bank cheque made payable to Virago for £ . . . .
☐ Please charge £ . . . . . . to my Visa/Delta/Maestro

Expiry Date ☐☐☐☐   Maestro Issue No. ☐☐

NAME (BLOCK LETTERS please) . . . .

ADDRESS . . . .

. . . .

. . . .

Postcode . . . . Telephone . . . .

Signature . . . .

Please allow 28 days for delivery within the UK. Offer subject to price and availability.